KU-444-813

MRS NELLIGAN'S PROPOSAL

The Major went an interesting shade of reddish-purple. He couldn't believe his ears.

'Are you suggesting that we use the Gun Club lands to build your damned complex on?' he croaked.

'Why not?' replied Mrs Nelligan. 'As I recollect, it is common land, going back several centuries and, I think, was originally held by the owners of the Castle before they returned to Britain after the Normans left. I am not quite sure just how Hackstown Gun Club managed to acquire it, but I feel sure that the members would be prepared to hand it over for the greater good.'

'Not on your bloody life, madam,' barked the Major, his neck swelling to such an extent that his wife's hopes of becoming a widow before she was too old to enjoy the change, were almost realised.

Also by Dolores Rockett in Sphere Books:

KNOCKPEDDAR & THE SWEET LIFE

Hackstown and the High Life

DOLORES ROCKETT

SPHERE BOOKS LIMITED

First published in Great Britain by
Sphere Books Ltd, 1986
27 Wright's Lane, London W8 5SW
Copyright © Dolores Rockett, 1986

Publisher's Note

This novel is a work of fiction. Names, characters, places and
incidents are either the product of the author's imagination or
are used fictitiously, and any resemblance to actual persons,
living or dead, events, or locales is entirely coincidental.

For My Mother

TRADE
MARK

This book is sold subject to the condition that
it shall not, by way of trade or otherwise, be lent,
re-sold, hired out or otherwise circulated without
the publisher's prior consent in any form of
binding or cover other than that in which it is
published and without a similar condition
including this condition being imposed on the
subsequent purchaser.

Set in Times

Printed and bound in Great Britain by
Cox & Wyman Ltd, Reading

Chapter One

Within one month of having accepted the retirement colour television and the statutory wallet of notes, Mrs Agnes Nelligan discovered a major fact of life: retirement was dead boring. What made the situation more unpalatable was that the people most vociferous about the joys of doing one's own thing – having plenty of time for leisure at last, being free to choose one's activities – were all people well and obviously happily entrenched in the full employment trap, and all of them seemed to be light-years away from that wonderland on the sidelines which they were now loudly advocating.

And it was not as if Mrs Nelligan was over the industrial hill. Had it not been for the fact that a galloping building development had closed the small but outrageously expensive Academy for Young Gentlemen, where she had reigned as Headmistress for the last fifteen years of a successful teaching career, Mrs Nelligan would not now be pottering round her minute garden, hoovering round her minute cottage, and writing her minute grocery list every day, when she could have been forging all those paths to the executive suites in the skyscrapers of commerce and capitalism, so that her 'boys' could continue to do her credit. And in forty years of teaching, Mrs Nelligan was proud to point out that with only a few exceptions (that wayward boy who later made such vulgar headlines in the theatrical publications, less for his thespian talent than for his sexual deviations was one she closed her memory to) all Mrs Nelligan's 'boys' went from her care to dizzy heights of public service, in high finance, politics, the Church, organised crime, learning and double dealing of one kind or another, in one country or another, and she was

1

inordinately proud of every last one of them – including, if she was truly honest with herself, even the one into deviations. At least it showed he wasn't afraid to buck the system when the system needed the challenge. Now, of course, she was reminded on occasion when yet another headline caught her eye in the newsagent's, deviation was no longer exotically Bloomsbury, but rather more mundanely Blackpool, and you couldn't get much more vulgar than *that* in Mrs Nelligan's view.

So here she was, a mere sixty, languishing in a cottage in the village of Hackstown with absolutely nothing to keep her mind occupied, her awareness exercised, her curiosity ticking comfortably over, and her ability to push events into conformity with all the strength and accuracy of a steam roller, going completely to waste. She missed the cut and thrust of school life, governors' meetings and the out-manoeuvring of her pupils, whose fathers before them had also failed to beat her at a game of one-upmanship in which, had there been diplomas handed out, Mrs Nelligan would have totally cornered the market.

Generations of small boys had ever been convinced that Mrs Nelligan had a third eye set somewhere off-centre in the back of her head, and a pet tabby cat who, they assured each other in delicious terror, was able to talk to her after midnight every Friday, so that she would know all their hidden misdemeanours in time for the Saturday morning Assembly in the Hall, when Reckoning time arrived. The senior pupils had good cause to be grateful to her when, after surviving her disciplines, they found that six years of Mrs Nelligan's care and methods more than equipped them for the worst that the world could launch at them in business, love or success, so that when it came to placing their own young out to be tarred with the same parental brush, it was unthinkable that anyone other than Agnes Nelligan would do the painting.

At the beginning of each new school year, parents of existing pupils would watch with a delight that even a rising stock market graph could not excel, the gentle fluttering of Mrs Nelligan among the guardians of the new boys. She would perch herself on the broad steps of the school, rosy cheeked, slender enough to almost pass for skinny, in her brown skirt and blouse, looking like a bemused robin, and standing, as her late husband was wont to say fondly, 'heart high' in her cuban-heeled brogue shoes, her brown eyes wide and seeming slightly puzzled at what they were looking at. Her whole appearance seemed to exude a conviction that life was a great big tapestry which might at any second descend over her small body and swamp her. Experienced parents knew only too well that Mrs Nelligan's timidity concealed a steely determination to achieve whatever she had in mind, and absolutely no compunction whatever when it came to using the influences and talents of all the Young Gentlemen who passed through her hands over her teaching career. And had any of them been interested in psychology, they might have read more than a little into the addition of a shocking pink silk scarf, somewhat rakishly knotted at her throat, its ends secured at the shoulder by a diamond brooch representing the god Janus, without which Mrs Nelligan was rarely seen abroad.

That same deceptive fluttering gained for the school a first-rate gymnasium, a library which was the envy of many a literary scholar, plus a yearly brief season of celebrity concerts and recitals in the Great Hall (Mrs Nelligan refused to .call it by any other title), a couple of major jazz clambakes for those with more downmarket tastes, among other little events, all of which were sponsored, provided, promoted and funded by the highly active and influential Parents' Committee.

She was, on her own part, equally generous in allotting the credit when opportunity arose.

'My goodness,' she would say gently, 'my boys deserve nothing less than the best because they *are* the best and their parents are well aware of the fact. Could we offer them something second-rate?'

It was a pity that industrialisation had encroached on the school environs to such an extent that the governors had decided the school would make three times the money if it were turned into a top-grade co-educational establishment for which the new rash of private housing schemes in the area had created a demand. Mrs Nelligan could not contemplate such a major change of direction – for one thing, she felt that teaching influence, to be totally effective, should not end at four o'clock in the afternoon. With reluctance, she decided to retire and return to her roots in Hackstown, where she had, over the years, maintained a cottage just outside the village.

Hackstown was a pretty place, even if it boasted of no more than a village square with a few streets leading off the main thoroughfare. It had, however, quite a pleasant if somewhat pretentiously named hotel, the Castle Court, which was run by Mr Matt Quinlan, a well-set man in his fifties. His ability to serve surprisingly excellent coffee was perfected during his stint with the British army in India. The Castle Court lounge was the meeting place for the morning drinkers, and those who had what might be loosely termed 'some standing' in the village. It included the President of the local Gun Club, a choleric red-nosed major named Mulqueen, whose compulsion to down-grade everyone he met, particularly Mr Quinlan, who was non-commissioned material, did not endear him to anyone, least of all his wife. When he could get away from the property world, which was every morning at eleven a.m. (he liked to give the lounge time to 'warm up'), another regular in the Castle Court was Mr William 'Billy' Markey, the local auctioneer. His firm occupied a prime site on the village square, and Billy looked after the affairs of most of the farming community, the big landowners and the retired well-to-do, in the district. He also happened to own the biggest public house and grain store in Hackstown, so what he missed hearing across his office desk, he caught up with over his taproom counter, so to speak. Indeed, many a good property deal came his way over an order for seed potatoes and a large whiskey.

And there were advantages going with the job. Billy was also Honorary Secretary of the Hackstown Golf Club. There, his ability to lose discreetly on the fourteenth hole on which there was a small pond that could, if you gauged the distance accurately, engulf a golf ball in its depths and give the opponent a two-stroke lead, also netted Billy many a sizeable commission.

Now that he was not meddling in the affairs of State, due

to his party's defeat in a recent general election, Charlie Donaghue, Hackstown's sitting member of government, spent his mornings in his own corner of the Castle Court lounge, where he could quietly cure his daily hangover without Major Mulqueen harassing him about the state of the nation. Charlie's chair was stationed within eye-catching distance of the bar, but behind a six-foot potted castor oil plant, which did very well in the lounge thanks to the regular dowsing Charlie gave it with the accompanying bottle of soda water he ordered with his morning double whiskey.

Then there were the Pearsons, Hackstown's bit of family quality, albeit impoverished. The Pearsons owned a wood-studded, run-down estate on the outskirts of Hackstown, where Geoffrey battled with sheep and their accompanying ailments, wresting a reluctant living from his acres; while his wife, a large-boned angular woman, bred labradors, ran their large, crumbling old mansion and kept paying guests in summer in surroundings which were low on little things like modern plumbing and telephonic communication, but high on antiques and atmosphere. They too, were regulars at the hotel, their only indulgence being the single glass of madeira sherry dallied over every morning before lunch.

Since her retirement, Mrs Nelligan had fallen into the habit of taking morning coffee at the hotel. The lounge had a single Gothic-shaped window at one end, a relic of the time when it was actually a part of the old castle chapel from which the hotel gained its name, and it was at a little wicker table by this window that Mrs Nelligan always sat – close enough to hear the conversation but far away enough not to be taken for one of the party of imbibers. Agnes was particular about the company she drank in.

On this particular June morning, she was at her usual spot. Finishing her coffee, she glanced out of the window, in time to see Charlie Donaghue drive into the hotel forecourt, in some considerable hurry. Agnes sensed something important was about to be related within minutes, so instead of leaving to pick up her dinner order at the butcher – with whom she carried on a running battle concerning an over-abundance of fat on her purchases – she poured the last dregs from the coffee pot and settled back in her chair. Charlie puffed his way to the counter and clutched a large hairy hand around the brandy that Matt Quinlan poured out, downing it in a single gulp and seizing the second which the proprietor silently placed before him, this time with the mandatory soda water alongside.

'You won't believe what I've just been told,' Charlie said breathlessly, as much from the trauma of what he was about to relate as from the jolt the brandy had given his system.

Mr Quinlan looked at him. 'I could tell you've had a bit of a shock, Mr Donaghue – I hope it's not a family tragedy?'

Charlie shook his head.

'Don't tell me that racehorse of yours is gone lame. You know the whole county has him backed to win on Saturday,' Billy Markey queried with some hope. Among his local interests, Billy was the major shareholder in the only bookmaking shop in Hackstown. It also serviced a twenty-mile radius of customers, so the money on Charlie's hopeful was all placed with his firm, and from what Billy heard in his pub, the only way 'Hackstown Lad' was going to lose the race was if he broke all four legs, developed vertigo and ran backwards during the event.

'Thank God, not that!' said Charlie. 'But what I'm going to tell you is damn near as drastic. The Hackstown Plastics factory is closing down in a month's time. And that means the bulk of the workforce in the area will be without jobs. I've just had a call from the shop steward who heard it this morning from the management.'

Everyone was silent. Hackstown Plastics, the village's only source of employment, produced a variety of items, ranging from plastic egg-boxes, watering cans and pull-along toys, to inflatable swimming rings, tap washers and a range of slightly phallic-looking garden stools. The company's activities and products were so diversified, it seemed inconceivable that the goods could no longer be assured of assimilation into a continually demanding world of consumerism. But there it was: rising costs, inflation, cut-backs in demand, taxes, wage levels – it could all, Charlie pointed out, be set to music. The question was now, what were they going to do about it?

It didn't take a university degree for the Hackstown locals to work out the repercussions of such a major closure. The village's sixteen pubs owed their existence to the factory wages, a fair share of which went into their cash registers every weekend and most week nights as well. The local snooker hall, the traders, the hotel itself, all supported or were supported by Hackstown Plastics Incorporated, and without the regular financial circulation, times might very well grow lean indeed. So they could see why Charlie Donaghue was even now downing his third double brandy in haste.

'Can't you do something, Mr Donaghue?' asked Mrs Pearson. 'After all, you are the Government representative for the area, even if your particular party is currently not the ruling one. I believe that is what political representatives are all about?'

'It's American money that runs Hackstown Plastics,' Charlie said glumly, 'and you can't deal with foreigners when the profit margin narrows down, as the rest of the country has also found out at one time or another. How many of them firms has upped and ran when things got sticky?'

'So you mean they are just going to pull out and leave Hackstown without any industry whatsoever?' Geoffrey Pearson asked.

'There isn't any choice – the company has ceased trading. Next month they'll wind down, and then – fare-thee-well!' Charlie replied.

'God damn it!' bellowed the Major. 'It would never have happened if the place had been properly run. The waste of money and manpower in that factory was appalling. Now, if the business were run on military lines . . .' Major Mulqueen was off on his favourite track. No one bothered to listen to him.

'Maybe the Government will take over the factory and continue to operate it,' Mrs Mulqueen suggested. Her husband immediately rounded on her.

'Don't be so damn stupid, woman! If the State moves in, what you get is twice the workforce, half the output and three times the inefficiency. No. What that place needs is proper management that will *tighten up the slack*.' Mrs Mulqueen sighed audibly. The Major spent his life urging the rest of the world to tighten up the slack. Sometimes she wished someone would do just that – around his bull neck.

'Well,' said Matt Quinlan, 'something will have to be done or else Hackstown is in trouble. There must be some way we can get new industry into the village. What about the EEC? They seem to be very ready to dish out cash for things.'

The Major snorted. 'Like travelling expenses for parliamentary members, I suppose,' he said. 'I'll bet that damn party of yours is busy creaming off those, along with anything else it can get its paws on.' Charlie glowered at him.

'Now then gentlemen, we won't get results by arguing about politics. What we want to think of is ways and means.' Matt Quinlan halted in its tracks what promised to turn into a high-powered slanging match.

The Major snorted again. 'Best leave such things to people with the professional expertise to evolve a workable programme,' he said loudly. 'It's not within the capabilities of the local talent to discover an equitable solution to such a major financial disengagement.'

Matt Quinlan reddened. 'Well now, Major, I recall that when the village needed a new Community Hall, it was the local talent among the people and the traders who got together a plan that raised the cash with which to build it! We didn't see much professional expertise around when it came to running sports and sales and raffles and weekly draws ... Mind you, the professionals were all up on the platform the day we had the Minister for Sports and Leisure Affairs down to Hackstown to declare the Hall officially open!'

In no little triumph, Matt resumed polishing the bar glassware while Mrs Mulqueen unsuccessfully drowned a titter with a quick sip of her sherry. She remembered only too well, as did Matt Quinlan, how the good Major had positioned himself alongside the Minister for the photo session and the speech making, resplendent in his army formals and medals, even though he had been loud in his opposition to the erection of the Hall, having blocked planning permission for it on two alternative sites, until the parish priest came up with a section of the church's private land, which was, unfortunately, right alongside the Major's garden. Now Major Mulqueen was compelled to listen to the thump of basket balls, the buzz of the women's meeting nights, the cacophony of disco sessions and, worst of all, the local brass and reed band's weekly practice, through the open windows of the Hall.

Mrs Nelligan listened with fascination. Her bright eyes moved from one to the other. There these men were, talking about formal protests, government intervention and someone to work a miracle, when what was really needed was a good functioning committee and a new plan of campaign to replace one work ethos with an alternative which would separate the commercial eggs into more than one basket. Diversification was an axiom she had been quite strong on when she taught the Sixth Form about business methods.

As she paid for her coffee, Mrs Nelligan was developing the glimmer of an idea. But she decided to work on it a little longer before she told the occupants of the Castle Court lounge about it. Agnes always believed in having her facts well marshalled, her parameters outlined and her back well defended before she went into combat; and this new battle – for a battle she knew it would be – was no different from the ones she had waged and won throughout her teaching career.

Chapter Two

As she cycled the half-mile back to her cottage, Mrs Nelligan thought what an attractive place the village was. Situated a mere sixty miles from the metropolis, Hackstown was smack in the middle of racing and hunting country without the factory development which she felt was rapidly destroying the beauty of the Irish rural countryside.

It had advantages like woodland, lakeland, good trout rivers, rolling countryside, neat stud farms, a fair share of archeological remains, and the village itself had an insularity and a rural arrogance which was invaluable when it came to retaining the scenic status quo. Not for Hackstown, then, the plastic-fronted take-aways, the space invader machines or the garish neon-sign world of the townships. The shopfronts were all carefully maintained in their Victorian splendour, complete with real canvas awnings in summer. The village square had its old stone horse trough, still faithfully filled with water by the local council even if no one brought a horse and cart into Hackstown any more. Mind you, the village had discovered the delights of Bingo, pub television and family planning, but all in the most discreet good taste. Hackstown was a place to relax in and it was this factor that Mrs Nelligan felt was going to be the real saving strength of the village.

One of the advantages of having the sons of successful capitalists under her care was the spin-off from the vacations bestowed by indulgent parents on the offspring, even if the educational and cultural levels were second-hand for her. Each autumn, Mrs Nelligan ran an essay competition for senior pupils, the prize being a golden key, slightly reminiscent of the American Phi Beta Kappa equivalent, only much more prized by the winner since there was only one of it awarded each year. The subject matter for the competition never varied: 'How I spent my Vacation', and through the activities of the contestants, which had to be written in considerable literary detail, Mrs Nelligan obtained an accurate not to say intimate knowledge of such diverse holiday pastimes as canoeing down the Amazon, climbing Mont Blanc, backpacking in darkest Africa, camel trekking across the Gobi desert, pub crawling in Paris, long-haul lorry driving in Australia and working a four-week stint in Disneyland, among other seasonal occupations enjoyed by her students.

It was the detailed account of the operations at Mr Disney's creation which now presented Mrs Nelligan with what she was sure was the perfect solution to Hackstown's problems. Here, she decided, would be the ideal location for a leisure complex designed on the same efficient lines as its American counterpart, but strictly Irish style. With the closure of the only factory in the area, there was now a local workforce ready and eager to turn its combined efforts to making a decent financial crust and this would keep the business in local hands for the most part. Agnes was not foolish enough to believe that Hackstown could go it completely alone.

She hurried through her evening meal, impatient to sit down at her desk and put her plan to paper. Many hours and many sheets of paper later, Mrs Nelligan completed her proposals and contentedly turning out her light, took herself to her bed where her plans for Hackstown took even more finite shape in her dreams, thereby sharpening up her concept in a highly detailed fashion. For when she recalled them after her alarm clock shrilled in a new day, her maxim of years concerning the advisability of sleeping on any major decision was, she felt with satisfaction, endorsed yet again.

At eleven fifteen precisely, Mrs Nelligan trotted into the lounge of the Castle Court Hotel, to her usual table in the window. Matt Quinlan brought over her tray of coffee and the two digestive biscuits Mrs Nelligan allowed herself each morning. She surprised him by ordering a small glass of his best Cointreau which she sipped in delicate mouthfuls

11

with her coffee, keeping a sharp ear to the conversation at the bar, as the regulars settled in for their morning session.

The Major, as usual, was complaining about the noise at night from the Community Hall which, he grumbled, would ultimately extend itself into the day time as well, once the factory finally closed its doors and the youth of Hackstown no longer had a job to go to.

'Those damned fellows will be down there banging snooker balls about or kicking footballs into my roses – either way, life will be insupportable. I tell you, if I wasn't so attached to my garden, I'd sell the damn house and move further out of Hackstown.'

Since it was Mrs Mulqueen who was responsible for every flower and blade of grass that grew in the place, the Major's reasons for remaining where he was were questionable at the least. Billy Markey, as the local auctioneer, was well aware that the Mulqueen bungalow was ready to collapse from dry rot, and that the annex foundations at the back of the house had already subsided a good foot ever since the Major, hoping to save on the construction costs, got a well-meaning but inexpert local handyman to build it on. Added to these small problems, the Major could not afford to move unless he sold the bungalow, and no one local was prepared to touch the place with a barge pole. The only time Billy got even a nibble of an offer for it, the stranger who looked it over unfortunately went to a pub other than Billy's for his farewell drink before leaving Hackstown, met with the drinkers in occupation, and was advised not to waste his cash on the Mulqueen residence. Which good counsel, needless to say, he acted upon.

'I rang a few friends in the city yesterday,' Charlie Donaghue reported.

'And?' asked Matt eagerly.

'They said they were fierce sorry for us but it wasn't anything new to hear,' replied Charlie sadly. 'They're getting the sob story ten times a day. And from the looks of things, there's likely to be another election which means that no one wants to put money into saving any business until they see what way the political cat will jump. After all, they want to be sure they're on the right side of the winning party line.'

Since that was the way Hackstown originally got its plastics factory, no one thought the attitude of the politically motivated big business concerns in any way unreasonable or immoral.

'I have often thought,' said Mrs Nelligan gently, 'That a rural community ought to be as autonomous as possible so that the wind of political change has little effect on its financial affairs.'

There was a small silence at the bar. It was the first time Mrs Nelligan had joined in the general conversation in all the months she had been frequenting the Castle Court lounge.

'That would be commendable, but difficult to achieve, I feel,' said Geoffrey politely.

'Nonsense, the little lady is quite right,' bellowed the Major. 'Any area could be its own boss if only people were prepared to put their backs into industry and tighten the slack. We've seen what outsiders can do to employment here in Hackstown, and next time let's hope we'll be wiser and come up with something that foreigners won't fold up on us at the drop of a baton.'

Mrs Nelligan fluttered at him as he flicked his moustache with what he erroneously imagined was a charismatic effect.

'I am so glad you agree with me, Major, because I've been giving the problem of the factory closure a little thought. Such a tragedy for all those young people who are working there . . .'

The Major raised his eyebrows and rolled a bloodshot eye at Geoffrey, the derisive gesture being unfortunately intercepted by Mrs Nelligan. Quite sharply for her, she whipped around.

'Tell me, Major, have you perhaps evolved some sort of workable idea which might be considered as a replacement for the factory? I am sure that with your military expertise solutions to problems like local unemployment will present themselves quite readily. The trained mind you know . . .' She smiled at the others and sipped again at her coffee. The Major spluttered into his drink.

Mrs Nelligan turned to Charlie Donaghue. 'You know, Mr Donaghue, when I was teaching and we offered our reference library facilities to the universities, after the parents had established it at my school, we found that the donations made by scholars who availed themselves of the library resources, were generous enough to keep the library self-supporting – in fact, it showed a little profit at the end of each year which somewhat offset the original cost of its establishment.'

Charlie nodded, still in some bewilderment at just where Mrs Nelligan's remarks were leading her.

'This is why I feel that a work source which is, shall I say, self-perpetuating, and which will not depend on the good graces of any particular political party, is the most suitable type of operation for a village such as Hackstown.'

Again Charlie nodded.

Mrs Nelligan put her head to one side reflectively. 'I have given the situation considerable attention in the past few days, and perhaps my plan might be worth consider-ation ...'

Again Mrs Nelligan took a bird-like sip from her Cointreau and, just as delicately, Mr Quinlan poured a refill into one of his best liqueur glasses and quietly placed it before her. A slight bow of her head acknowledged the gift as she patted her lips with a pale pink handkerchief.

'I think Hackstown could do very well if we were to establish a really top-class leisure centre catering for a variety of activities both indoor and outdoor. I visualise it as a sort of mixture of Gaelic Fairyland or Tir na n-Og, and the Ireland of ancient Celtic folklore – the Fianna, Deirdre, Cuchulain and so on. There would be the ancient beehive huts for visitors to live in during their stay. We could have re-enactments of the Children of Lir, who, as you will remember, were changed into swans, and they could swim on the lake and we could also stage regular water ballets. Tourists might like to go hunting with the Fianna or take trips with Granuaile. I have lots of suggestions and ideas for the complex and really it could well rival Disneyland, in an Irish context, of course. Foreigners, especially Americans, are always keen to get back to their roots ...'

Mrs Nelligan gazed out of the window. 'There would naturally be various spin-off advantages to such a venture, such as franchises, craft and souvenir sales and manufacture, contracts for supplies and so on. Really, it should prove quite profitable for the entire district and, of course, the local businessmen would certainly improve their current situation. And then there would be the usual things like fishing, shooting, boating on the lake in specially designed boats and little novelty things like leprechaun hunts – I think it might all be most entertaining, don't you?'

There was an awed silence in the lounge. The magnitude of what Mrs Nelligan was proposing was difficult to assimilate immediately. To a man, they moved to the bar, where Matt refilled each glass with Olympic speed, and then Billy, downing his whiskey, gave the idea his professional consideration.

'It'd take a power of money to set up, you know. Where will it all come out of? If the government is too skint to put money into the factory, they're not going to find the pot of gold all of a sudden for something like this.'

'I think that a good deal of the cost might be offset if we turned the complex into a co-operative as much as possible, and according to one of my boys who is something on the stock exchange, money can always be found for an original venture if one knows how to go about looking for it,' said Mrs Nelligan.

The Major smacked his lips and placed his glass on the counter with a pleased deliberation. What he saw as a chance to upstage Mrs Nelligan was not to be missed.

'There is only one factor you seem to have overlooked in all these admirable plans,' he said. 'You're talking about a sizeable section of land on which to put your leisure complex. Where is it going to come from at today's prices? Even if all the land in the area wasn't already agricultural land, you'll not buy it with the shillings and pence of a co-operative movement!' He guffawed loudly.

Mrs Nelligan sipped from her glass once more. Really, the Major was a most unlikeable man – he reminded her of the guardian of that nice Royston-Mainwaring boy. Now *him* she had suspected from the start and she later was instrumental in having him prosecuted for defrauding her pupil of a fair share of his inheritance.

'I envisage around two hundred acres, Major,' she fluted. 'But that should not prove a problem. We have nearly two hundred good acres of land not being fully utilised, as I recall. I believe only the Gun Club makes any use of it – and only in the shooting season.'

The Major went an interesting shade of reddish-purple. He couldn't believe his ears.

'Are you suggesting that we use the Gun Club lands to build your damned complex on?' he croaked.

'Why not?' replied Mrs Nelligan. 'As I recollect, it is common land, going back several centuries and, I think, was originally held by the owners of the Castle before they returned to Britain after the Normans left. I am not quite sure just how Hackstown Gun Club managed to acquire it, but I feel sure that the members would be prepared to hand it over for the greater good.'

'Not on your bloody life, madam,' barked the Major, his neck swelling to such an extent that his wife's hopes of becoming a widow before she was too old to enjoy the change, were almost realised.

'As President of the club, I state here and now that over my dead body will anyone take over the club shooting land. It's the best preserve in the county.'

'And kept for the exclusive use of a mere fifty people,' Mrs Nelligan murmured, as she buttoned her coat and prepared to leave.

'Since it is common land, it would not cost anything to acquire, and a great deal of money would be saved which could be utilised to improve the plans for the complex – as I pointed out, perpetuation,' she reminded the company as she departed.

Geoffrey looked after her as she disappeared round the corner of the building and out of sight.

'You know, she may have something in what she says,' he remarked. 'Can you see the tourist trade Hackstown could do, not only from the Irish side but the kind of overseas business we could envisage? I think we could make a damn fortune if we handled it all correctly and kept out

16

governmental interference, among a few other things.' He cast a quick look over at the Major who was still endeavouring to recover his temper in sufficient strength to vent his anger on his wife.

'The whole idea is unworkable and quite out of the question, and I for one would be completely against it,' said Major Mulqueen. 'Take over the Gun Club preserve indeed! The woman is fit to be committed – gone senile in her old age. Why, the members would never allow it.'

He slammed down his glass and stomped out. Mrs Mulqueen took her time. She smiled gently to herself as she touched up her lipstick in the ladies' cloakroom. Susan Mulqueen had the distinct feeling that the Major was about to have his entire lifestyle upended, and by a means he was not going to like very much. The more she considered Mrs Nelligan's timidity, the more she began to appreciate what the Gun Club might be up against. Indeed, she could almost feel sorry for her husband, who, she knew, was quite unable to come to terms with defeat at the hands of a female. But she felt with the certainty of a survivor who had weathered fifteen years of matrimony with a husband like Oliver Mulqueen, that Agnes would be the mouse who would trip up the elephant.

Back in his office, Billy Markey spent a useful hour going through his property register. For once, he was glad that the sales market for houses was experiencing a small slump, since it left him with a decent collection of desirable residences in the district which he looked forward to off-loading once the leisure complex got going. And like Mrs Mulqueen, Billy was quite sure it would all come about, just as Mrs Nelligan planned. He wasn't sure just why he believed in the project, but he did have a couple of major clients who, he knew, had once been under Mrs Nelligan's expert tuition and their almost religious respect for their headmistress had impressed him.

The Pearsons drove home in their ramshackle saloon with a combined feeling of exhilaration. Geoffrey quickly realised that his land bordered the acres used by the Gun Club and that there was bound to be some advantage accruing from its proximity. Majorie Pearson had thought of something which she felt was going to prove a real little goldmine to them. Marjorie was planning to go into the antiques business. She had a sizeable collection of family bits and pieces in the house, most of which she loathed, her own taste leaning heavily toward modern Swedish. With raftloads of foreign tourists almost over her garden fence, so to speak, here was the perfect way to replace the lot with the kind of furniture she had yearned over in the furnishing magazines, and make a tidy profit while she did so. The mews at the back of the courtyard would, she thought, make an excellent shop and storeroom – she might even hire a couple of carpentry students from the local school to do basic furniture repairs, and she was quite good at upholstery herself. God knows, with the way their money was over the past years, she had plenty of practice making do with what they had, she sighed. And she could at last give up the thankless job of being a summer landlady, obliged to smile her way through one exhausting day after another, coping with the spills and horrors of outrageous children from June to September each year. By which it can be gathered that Mrs Pearson infinitely preferred her dogs to juvenile humanity, and with good reason, she would remark. It simply wasn't done to shove an incontinent baby's foot in the inevitable results of two helpings of warm milk, and besides this, the puppies were faster learners than toddlers.

And suddenly she had an even more brilliant idea: visitors with pets, to whom the laws of quarantine would not apply, who would patronise the complex, might also be happy to have their animals take holidays with them, except that Marjorie would provide an upmarket boarding service with all the expertise which twenty years of rearing her labradors could offer. And right alongside the complex for easy visiting, into the bargain.

Her mind soared into dizzy heights of planning. She visualised a luxury kennels with gourmet menus, sprung beds, doggie loos and tapestry scratching chairs for all the lucky feline clients who might take advantage of the de luxe accommodation. She saw a succession of rich owners queuing at the gates of Hackstown House to engage rooms for their pets while they sported themselves in the complex and returned to the ancient Gaelic pastimes of the natives.

When she talked her ideas over with Geoffrey, he was just as enthusiastic; anything that would alter their combined way of life and release him from his commitment to the two hundred sheep whose talent was manifest for developing liver fluke, foot rot, worms, ticks, mouth ulcers, toothache and general collywobbles, usually on the most freezing days of the winter, was all right by him.

In a moment of wild abandonment, the Pearsons made up their minds to invest what was left of Marjorie's inheritance from her grandfather, into the co-operative, and in the meantime to have a word with Geoffrey's brother Julian, who had connections in the world of architecture. After all, they told each other firmly, if one were about to launch into a new project such as a kennels fit to be used by the pets of film stars, executives and even the royals of the Arab world, then a little expert professional advice on how to construct the place without having the stables fall down around one's ears – what with the dry rot and the woodworm – would not go amiss.

It was mid-afternoon before Mrs Nelligan managed to contact one of her 'old boys', one Percival 'Pidgie' Roberts, whose expertise in genealogical matters had obtained for him a senior position at one of the country's major universities.

'Pidgie dear,' she told him, having got the pleasantries out of the way, 'I have a few dates and things I want you to check out for me concerning a parcel of land here in Hackstown. I seem to recall that we did a little local genealogical survey once when you were in the Sixth Form and you came across some interesting facts about that particular tract.'

Percival settled back in his chair. 'Are you about to become a landowner, dear Mrs Nelligan?' he asked.

Mrs Nelligan's voice sounded reproving from the other end of the connection. Percival was immediately back in her study, the years of intellectual success falling away in a second.

'Don't treat it lightly, Percival. The request is a serious one and I need the information in great detail and in somewhat of a hurry, so please put your attention to it immediately, there's a good boy. It is urgent to establish ownership, and when you do so, I can then explain to you what my request is about.'

She listed her requirements and Percival made copious notes, promising to send her on the results of his investigations as soon as he turned up the information. Meantime, Mrs Nelligan made a few preparations of her own.

She suddenly thought she would enjoy a little holiday.

Chapter Three

It was a week later that 'Pidgie' Roberts's bulky envelope was delivered to Mrs Nelligan by registered post – a fact which interested Con Doolin, the Hackstown postman, since it was not common practice for missives with seals, and imposing looking literary logos imprinted on them, to drop into his delivery bag, as it were. Governmental communications, from a variety of departments, were not worthy of a second examination. They were usually, Con found, either tax demands, final notices to the telephone subscribers, refusals from the Social Welfare division or, in Charlie Donaghue's case, publicity documents and Government reports which the Civil Servants quite erroneously expected their government representatives would read and assimilate in their spare time.

The envelope was stamped as having emanated from the 'Department of History and Genealogy' which may have accounted for the strong rumour that later went through Hackstown, that Mrs Nelligan had discovered an historic 'dig' at the back of her cottage, and was about to invest in a metal detector to help her unearth an ancient treasure valuable enough to rival the Ardagh chalice.

Pidgie had gone to considerable trouble on her behalf. Not only had he done a complete written investigation but he had also included a well-documented family tree and he had actually turned up a couple of crumbling land deeds from sources only he knew about. She studied the documents carefully. 'My,' she said with some satisfaction. 'Fancy Pidgie being able to trace the name back to an early king of Leinster. That will prove most acceptable. It quite outweighs the fact that the great-great-grandfather's brother was hanged as a sea pirate and the great-grandfather known as the cleverest rum runner in the West Indies. How fortunate that I persuaded Percival where his talents lay when he was with the Sixth Form group. He would never have been successful as a professional racing driver, as he must now surely realise!'

Over the years of her teaching career, Mrs Nelligan had enjoyed a fascinating hobby. She kept a complete rundown on her past pupils and her filing system faithfully recorded their career progress, job changes, company acquisitions, marriages, offspring, divorces, mistresses (where the information came into her possession), ups and downs, successes and failures. In fact, her system was far superior to those of such bureaucracies as MI5, the Foreign Office, the Police, the FBI, Interpol and even the CIA. She had bits of information which would have been much appreciated by these bodies had they been privy to a number of the files of some of her old boys. It was one of her major pleasures, keeping her indexes up to date, particularly when the tedium of retirement descended, so that it took only an hour of her time to work out a solid working list of 'boys' who would prove helpful when she began the business of organising the Hackstown Tir na n-Og plans.

Her confidence grew as she made her way through the village to do her shopping. The grapevine had been in operation and the citizens of Hackstown were encouragingly enthusiastic about the proposed complex, even if their knowledge of the details was sketchy.

'I hear you know someone who knows someone who might be openin' up a brewery here,' commented the butcher as he carefully removed every last vestige of fat from Mrs Nelligan's quarter-pound of best steak before weighing it.

'They tell me your brother will be looking for two hundred workers when he starts building them fork-lift trucks in his garage down the road,' said Mrs Devlin, as she wrapped Agnes's order of apples and pears in layers of tissue paper, off-handedly popping in a complimentary bunch of purple grapes in a corner of the box.

'Aren't we fortunate you know someone up there in Dublin? I hear we might be getting a handout from the

Social Fund,' commented Johnnie Fennessey, the sole custodian of the law and order prevailing in Hackstown, as he helped Mrs Nelligan with her bicycle and basket when she met him on her way into the Castle Court Hotel.

Mrs Nelligan looked surprised. 'Really,' she said, 'I don't know where all the stories emanated from. I am hoping to do a little something to alleviate Hackstown's unemployment problems, but whether or not I will succeed is still open to question. One cannot be assured of the backing of the entire village.'

'Aye, so I heard,' said Guard Fennessey. 'But Hackstown needs jobs more than grouse, and if I thought withdrawing every gun licence in the district would be of any help to you, then that is exactly what I'd do!'

Mrs Nelligan looked suitably shocked. 'Dear me,' she trilled. 'I don't really think that procedure will be necessary. One can always prevail on people to see sense if one only has a little patience and understanding. And of course, if one also knows the correct buttons to push!' And she trotted to her usual table in the lounge.

The Major strutted up to her as she sat down. 'The news is just as I expected,' he said. 'We had a meeting of the club committee on Sunday morning. The vote was unanimous to preserve the club lands in the status quo. You'll have no luck at all trying to persuade the committee to vote your way – they all agree the members would never stand for it. Anyway, the grouse season will be opening. Members have parties arranged for. I'm expecting my usual group of Top Brass down and they've got used to the annual shoot, just as we all have.'

'I expect your current season will remain unaffected for this year, Major,' said Mrs Nelligan gently. 'But I would hesitate to make any long-term plans – one should never look too far ahead in these uncertain times, as one of my old boys who is now in the work study profession, always tells me. It saves considerable disappointment later on if one extends one's planning period to a forseeable parameter.'

She smiled slightly at him. 'I heard you were endeavouring to expand the membership of the Gun Club through a plan which will enable members to avail of facilities for a

23

five-year period at a time if they are prepared to pay a lump sum. And I understand that with the capital thus raised, the committee is planning to build a club house with a bar and restaurant for the use of club members – or am I mistaken?' She widened her blue eyes at Major Mulqueen.

The Major blinked. He had believed that no one outside of himself and the Gun Club Vice-President, a well-heeled business executive who lived in the city and only resided in the environs of Hackstown at weekends, and then only in the shooting season, were aware of the plans afoot for the Gun Club.

'I would not make too many commitments on that one, Major – it is so embarrassing when one has to admit a failure to deliver!'

She nodded at him with a polite indication of dismissal, and had the Major been a more sensitive soul, he would have been reminded of his cadet days in the army when his C.O. gave precisely the same movement of the head after a dressing-down had been administered.

Matt Quinlan who had overheard the exchange was doing a slow burn behind his bar. As the Major made a hurried excursion into the men's room, Matt angrily clattered the pint glasses.

'Isn't he the cute con man all the same, now, planning a scheme like that without telling a soul?' he said bitterly to Billy Markey. 'Talk about taking the bread out of the mouths of the needy! My God, the last thing I need in Hackstown is another bar and restaurant going up to compete for the few bob I can scrape in over and above the rest of the local publicans. Sure, if I didn't do the lunch trade, I could close the hotel for half the year, and there's no doubt that during the season I get all the business from the Gun Club crowd. If Mulqueen and his committee put up a restaurant, the members would use that and I could shut the shop completely.'

'Well,' said Billy reflectively, 'maybe it would be as well so if Mrs Nelligan's idea does come to something. You could expect a real profitable spin-off from a leisure complex, couldn't you?'

'I could at that,' replied Matt with a distinct lightening of his mood. By a slightly convoluted system of progressive thought, it had occurred to him that the Gun Club's lands, composed of bogland, hilly country, wooded stretches, some marshland and a rather scenic lake area, none of which was capable of sustaining anything more than the wildlife the members so enthusiastically butchered during the shooting season, were a couple of miles from the village. The complex would ultimately need a commuting service for visitors, and Matt was determined he would operate it, with naturally, its departure and arrivals point being the courtyard of the Castle Court Hotel. There, Mr Quinlan decided, he would have a patio area with tables for waiting drinkers, a coffee and sandwich service, even an ice-cream booth for the children, and who knows what other innovations once he put his mind to the project. And at that precise moment, he suddenly loved the whole world and was even, temporarily, prepared to tolerate the Major who was now back in the lounge, still trying to work out where Mrs Nelligan had managed to discover what he had believed to be the best-kept secret since he and a brother officer had tied the C.O.'s wife's knickers to the camp flagpole the day they got their first posting out of training.

As Mrs Nelligan left the lounge, she stopped to chat with Mrs Mulqueen on the way out.

'I do hope the geraniums you kindly gave me will do well, dear Mrs Mulqueen. I cannot hope to be as excellent a gardener as you are, but perhaps one day when you are passing, you might call in and see how the plants are progressing?'

Mrs Mulqueen nodded. 'You will find they will do very well with you. Just keep them nicely watered and feed them properly, and do remember the things I told you – about garden pests and frost, of course.' Mrs Mulqueen looked squarely into Mrs Nelligan's eyes and the merest suspicion of a wink passed between them both.

'I shall be away on a short holiday for about ten days, Mr Quinlan,' said Mrs Nelligan as she settled her bill. 'And when I return, I hope to have some definite news which will set things moving in the right direction.'

'And where were you thinking of going, ma'am?' asked Matt.

'To the United States of America,' replied Mrs Nelligan. 'I thought I would visit my niece in New York and of course so many of my old boys are working and living throughout the United States, and they have on many occasions invited me to visit with them. This seems an ideal time to avail myself of the many invitations I have received. I shall discuss our problems with them and, who knows, I may find the answers we need.'

'I've always wanted to go there myself,' Matt said. '"The land of opportunity" they call it, don't they? I'll bet your lads have done very well for themselves out there over the years. You won't want for anything when you visit them.'

Mrs Nelligan nodded somewhat proudly. So many of her 'boys' had made the grade quite nicely: there was Ambrose out there on the West Coast with a major television studio to his name, not to mention Andrew who was rather important in railways, as she recalled, and Matthew who did so well in films, and that quiet boy Madison, who afterwards became a real dynamo, they told her, in the theatrical world of America. Who would have thought that his days of directing the school drama group would have led him into the world of impresarios in New York! She shook her head admiringly. And she would certainly enjoy staying with David who owned that enormous cattle-ranch, and she had also promised Allan to come and see his oil wells – though what she could say about an oil well that would sound complimentary, she simply could not imagine.

Then she regarded Mr Quinlan, whose total discretion was almost a cause of resentment among the more gossipy members of Hackstown village, and she took a decision.

'Mr Quinlan, I have a particular purpose in visiting America at this time. I want you to read this document and then I will explain my idea to you.' She produced the envelope with the results of Pidgie's labours contained therein, and gave it to Matt to study. When he had finished, she outlined her plans and when his delighted laughter had subsided, they had a serious discussion which left both of them satisfied that Mrs Nelligan had a viable idea.

There was only one small snag in her plans. Time being of the essence, Mrs Nelligan had elected to take the plane to America rather than her preferred method of going by ship to whatever destination she happened to have in mind at any holiday period. It would be her first time to travel by air, and she regarded the whole prospect with some trepidation. It still seemed quite ridiculous to her that anyone would lock themselves into a steel tube, no matter how well lined it might be inside, and travel, suspended in nothingness, from one place to another by some means known only to God, science and ornithology. She quite understood the principles; it was the practice she found unacceptable.

It was as much through anxiety about being late for her flight, as a fear that she would chicken out at the last moment and not catch the plane at all, that had Mrs Nelligan at the airport a couple of hours in advance of her official checking-in time.

In the coffee bar where she was putting in the time before her boarding call, Agnes had a conversation with one of the ground hostesses who was sharing her table. It was to change her entire plan pattern had she but known.

The young woman in question had a secret ambition to rise to even higher things than manning the check-in desks in the airport, like becoming head of the Consumer Relations Department, for starters. A quick check revealed Mrs Nelligan's transatlantic ticket folder, while her slightly harried glances and involuntary nervous jumps every time the public address system announced another boarding instruction, told the experienced hostess that here was a first-time passenger, obviously travelling alone, judging by the unpaid bill for a single pot of coffee which lay on her side plate.

She smiled at Agnes in the 'now-there's-no-need-to-worry-even-though-the-plane-is-slightly-on-fire' manner which is the first procedure taught to all airline personnel, ground based or airborne.

'Is this your first trip to America?' she asked sweetly.

'My first trip in an aeroplane, actually,' replied Mrs Nelligan apologetically, feeling suddenly rather old fashioned.

'Really?' asked the young woman with interest. 'What *have* you been doing with yourself?'

'Teaching school and retiring – in that order,' laughed Mrs Nelligan, quite unoffended. 'I simply preferred to travel by sea – people sometimes do, you know!'

The hostess sniffed. 'Flying is the only way to go,' she said, and then giggled as she thought of the implications of what she had just said. Mrs Nelligan too, had grasped the drift.

'I do hope not,' she said with a nervous little smile. 'My niece Katie would be so disappointed if I don't get to New York after all. She has arranged to take her vacation to coincide with my visit.'

'What does your niece do in New York?' the hostess enquired, still hoping to find an interesting story in Mrs Nelligan which she could pass along to Consumer Relations to add to the growing list she telephoned in every week.

'Well,' said Mrs Nelligan even more apologetically, 'she owns a rather well-known boutique chain. You may have heard of it – "Katinka's"? She designs things.'

The hostess stared at her. A decent story at last! She could hardly wait to get the details before finding an internal telephone.

'You mean that famous chain is owned and run by your niece? But Katinka is supposed to be a Russian noblewoman, according to the American fashion magazines. I know that all the famous Hollywood stars and leading personalities have their clothes designed by Katinka. She's been called America's challenge to Dior.'

'When she was little, Katie always enjoyed making doll dresses – that is until her brothers talked her into taking up cricket instead of sewing,' said Mrs Nelligan reminiscently. 'She was a great little batsman.'

'Then she's not really Russian at all?' said the hostess.

'Good heavens no! She was born in County Leitrim – her father used to be Head of Police Administration in New York until he had rather a stupid accident which proved

28

fatal – he tripped over the family dog and fell down the porch steps. James always had more brawn than brains. He weighed eighteen stone when he fell and most of the weight was around his waistline, so he didn't even see the dog before he fell over it.'

The ground hostess hurried off to make her telephone call and within minutes was back with a staff photographer and a courtesy executive who removed Mrs Nelligan to the rooftop gardens for a photographic session and a glass of complimentary wine, with the good wishes of the airline's public relations division. It was all extremely flattering, except that the ground hostess quite forgot that Mrs Nelligan was an intending passenger, so that when she delicately suggested she should now be moving into embarkation to catch her flight, a slightly horrified silence descended on the group. High in the sky, a jumbo jet whined its way over the airport and the executive had a check of his watch.

'I'm afraid – we've – er – caused you to miss your flight, madam,' he told her. 'It has just left.'

Two hours later, with only her hand baggage in her possession, since her heavy luggage had already disappeared into the wild Irish sky on the earlier jumbo (and which never again came to hand though the airport authorities vainly searched over four airports for the brown pigskin suitcase which contained her sensible fairisle jumpers and checked tweed skirts), Mrs Nelligan was seated in the luxury section of a New York-bound jet by courtesy of an apologetic executive of the Irish airlines, in surroundings a far cry from the package-priced flight she had originally booked herself.

And as she settled into her seat, she studied the other passengers, wondering as they moved up the aisle which of them would be sharing the window seat beside her own. And she was more than pleased to see her travelling companion was going to be a tall and singularly handsome young man with wide-set grey eyes, a humorous mouth and a shock of curly blond hair that wandered over his coat collar in a manner which, had she been his headmistress, Mrs Nelligan would have insisted be properly barbered.

That, plus a couple of buttons missing from his somewhat crumpled shirt, and a small tear in the sleeve of his jacket, told her he was probably in need of care and attention from a loving woman. And for some unknown reason, she recalled that so far as she was aware, Katie had, up to now, said she was far too busy with her career to indulge in any romantic involvements.

Chapter Four

The young man tossed a somewhat overloaded duffle bag and a large camera case into the storage compartment overhead, flopped down into the seat beside Mrs Nelligan and smiled widely.

'Hi there,' he said. 'My name is Jonathan Hogan and I guess we are going to be companions as far as New York.' Mrs Nelligan shook the proffered hand which gripped hers firmly without bruising her small fingers (a point immediately in Mr Hogan's favour, since a career of shaking hands when greeting parents had taken its toll on her knuckle joints) and smiled back.

'It would seem so,' she replied. 'And no doubt I will be hanging on to your sleeve once we take off. This is my first flight.'

'Be my guest,' said Jonathan hospitably. 'I know exactly how you feel – I went through the same thing when I took my first trip. In fact, every time I do something the first time around, I get the same feeling that I've left my stomach somewhere else and have to wait for it to catch up with me.'

'Your job offers variety then?' Mrs Nelligan probed gently, being far too discreet to ask outright how Mr Hogan made his crust.

'You could say that,' said Jonathan clipping his safety belt in place and automatically leaning over to help Mrs Nelligan fasten hers. 'I work for a television company and I've just been over here in Ireland working on a documentary programme. We took an average American tourist family and followed them around the country on a fourteen-day tour, except that we took in the offbeat spots as well as Connemara and Killarney and I think the result is going to be good. I found spots I had never read about and,

31

believe me, all those odd local items and the archeological remains were really something! Ireland is a country of oddities – and I don't mean the people!'

'What a pity you never reached my village during your travels,' said Mrs Nelligan with some regret. 'Hackstown is full of atmosphere and unusual features. Now, if you were interested in megalithic remains, Ogham stones, ancient burial grounds and pre-Christian ruins, then I do regret you were unaware of the existence of Hackstown. Why, we have had Japanese archeologists investigating our beehive huts which are regarded as among the finest examples of the period, which are in existence.'

'Well, I guess we'll be back again anyhow, so I'll make a point of catching the place,' said Jonathan, settling back as, without much more than a shudder, the plane began to taxi down the runway. While Mrs Nelligan was searching in her handbag for the glucose sweet she had been given by the hostess and had immediately dropped in among the smelling salts, the travel pills and cologne refresher pads without which she never went very far, they were airborne and on their way.

'You know,' she confided as they unclipped their seat belts and Jonathan lit a cigarette, 'it was actually the take-off I was scared off. Once one is up there, there isn't much point in thinking about it or the consequences of a mishap – is there?'

Jonathan laughed. 'Do you apply that attitude to everything else you do?' he asked.

'Why not? Once you take on something you then become committed, and starting to worry as to the eventual outcome is self-destructive. One must go on with a firm belief that it will eventually turn out as one plans. That is what I always advised my boys. Think positively and soldier on.'

'And did they?'

'Most decidedly. You probably know or have heard of many of them professionally and socially.'

She proceeded to give Jonathan a rundown of some of her 'boys' which left him observing her with a new-found respect.

32

'Your name comes from one of the great Gaelic families,' she told Jonathan as, having battled their way through the assembly-line meal, which left no reminder on the palate and whose only claim on the memory was the momentary occupation of working out what the foil tray actually contained, they were sipping their coffees. 'Does your family have an Irish connection?'

'Not so as you'd notice,' replied Mr Hogan happily. 'I tell people, I'm actually a little different because I'm not coming to Ireland to find my roots. My father was born in Nebraska, his father was born in New York, and before that the family settled in New England. Great grand-daddy was Polish!'

'Then, where did your name come from?' enquired Mrs Nelligan with some curiosity.

'Well,' said Jonathan, 'my Dad actually adopted it years ago for business purposes. He thought it sounded better on television than Zabelitzki. He does a TV talk show called *Hogan's Hello*. It goes out coast to coast five evenings a week. Top ratings too.' Jonathan was justly proud of his parent.

'How interesting,' said Agnes. 'Then he must know one of my old boys – 'Bobo' Carter – he has an interest in WCTTI. Dear Ambrose, he was forever fussing about with his ham radio when I had him in Fourth Year. I was so pleased to see he put his hobby to such good use when he returned to America. Even if he did regularly short circuit the electrical systems at school!'

Jonathan swallowed. President of one of the country's leading television organisations wasn't exactly amateurs-ville, particularly when your family also held the controlling stock interest, plus a sizeable piece of the spin-off industries of the parent company.

'Mr Ambrose Carter is quite a wheel in TV circles,' he told her and Mrs Nelligan nodded without too much interest.

She rummaged through her handbag and came up with a photograph. 'This is my niece Katie. I will be spending some time with her in New York,' she said, passing the photo to Jonathan. He stared at the picture and suddenly felt as though someone had thumped him hard on the back of his

33

neck. He went slightly dizzy, his throat quite unaccountably dried up because his Adam's apple felt as though it had swelled to unacceptable proportions and a light dew broke out under his eyes – sensations to which it must be said Mr Hogan was no stranger. Except that he usually associated them with a lengthy hangover or a bout of flu, but certainly not with occurring after a single glance at a picture of the most beautiful girl he had ever been privileged to see.

'She l-lives in N-New York?' he croaked unbelievingly, for how could such a creature exist on his own home patch without his having come across her in the street or anywhere? He was quite convinced that such a goddess was earmarked for a fine upstanding blond Caucasian such as himself, and heaven help whatever guy she was with when Jonathan met and ultimately but definitely won her.

Mrs Nelligan nodded, quite satisfied with the effect the photograph was obviously having on the young man. It was time Katie settled down and started rearing a couple of sons, she decided. This career business was fine but it was best left to the women whose matrimonial assets, looks and charm were a little more behind the eightball than a beauty like her dear Katie.

'She'll be meeting me at the airport, unless of course, she gets tied up and sends someone else to do so,' she said casually, settling back in her seat and closing her eyes. All of which left Jonathan to chew his lip for the rest of the trip in a panic of anxiety in case Katie didn't make the airport and he would lose his chance to be introduced to her.

He stuck closer to Mrs Nelligan than her tweed jacket and skirt, and insisted in taking charge of her hand luggage as they made their way towards the main concourse at Kennedy.

He hurriedly waved away the rest of his camera crew, made rapid promises to his assistant to turn up at his office by nine a.m. on the morrow (which rather surprised her, since the following day was a Sunday) and, taking Mrs Nelligan by the elbow, he rushed her into the main hall.

His efforts were rewarded. 'There she is, there's Katie!' Mrs Nelligan began to wave vigorously and with a flurry of what Jonathan later discovered was a voluminous cloak of turquoise-blue wool, a tall slim girl swept towards them and enveloped Mrs Nelligan in a massive hug.

'Darling Aunt Agnes, how marvellous to have you here at last,' cried the vision, planting smacking kisses on Mrs Nelligan's pink cheeks and then turning her dazzling smile on a completely bemused Jonathan who stood there clutching a bulging shocking pink canvas holdall and a large brown leather handbag on a gilt chain which Mrs Nelligan now took from his grasp.

'This is Jonathan Hogan. He's in television and so is his father, Katie dear. He has been so kind to me on the flight – I never found the time to be nervous because he kept me entertained all the way to New York,' she told her niece.

'How kind,' said Katie vaguely, her attention occupied with finding the remainder of her aunt's luggage. Jonathan instantly volunteered to search the baggage department while they waited for him in the bar. After a vain search for over an hour, they gave up on the brown suitcase until later. By then Jonathan was, he felt, a small bit further on in his plan to advance his pursuit of Katie O'Carroll.

'Don't worry about your clothes, Aunt Agnes. I can fix you up from the shop,' Katie said consolingly, as Jonathan returned finally, to admit a total failure to find anything resembling the Nelligan luggage in the forward baggage sections.

'Chances are the baggage is on its way to Hong Kong by now,' he said.

Mrs. Nelligan was horrified. 'Not on an Aer Lingus aeroplane surely,' she said; and then with justifiable recall, 'well, perhaps you may be right. If they could manage to forget me on a New York flight, what could they not do with my baggage?'

'Some day,' said Jonathan with an experienced air, 'you will walk down a street in somewhere like Saigon, and there will be your best Aran gansey, flaunting itself on some young lad pulling a rickshaw!'

He gathered up Mrs Nelligan's holdall and jacket and escorted them to the airport taxi rank where he handed them into a waiting cab, despite their protests – well, Katie's at any rate, since Mrs Nelligan was quite happy to hang on to Jonathan for as long as she decently could, to give him a fighting chance of arranging a date with her niece. Agnes had decided Jonathan would make an ideal husband for Katie, who, she told herself, would only have to be told a few times until she would see the obvious advantages of falling in love with a handsome young man on his way up the professional ladder. Agnes liked him, and she was too experienced not to trust her initial impressions. So she flustered more than usual, until Jonathan had installed himself in the front of the cab and elicited Katie's home address for the driver to take them to. Once they reached the apartment, Katie would have seemed churlish had she not invited Jonathan in for a coffee. Anyway, he was by that time halfway up the steps with her aunt's belongings over his shoulder, while he manfully struggled with his own gear as well.

While Katie showed her aunt to her room, Jonathan looked round the lounge whose windows curved outwards to overlook Central Park, and from which he could now watch the early-evening traffic moving far below. The room itself was long and full of pale tonal effects: dove grey walls; full creamy tweed curtains at the windows; sink-into settees covered in matching tweed, sparkled by big cushions covered in scarlet and grey silk; low-set mahogany tables whose wood gleamed with the sheen only acquired by constant and loving care and regular polishing (much later when they were on more intimate terms, he discovered that Katie used an old Irish trick of kerosene and turpentine sprinkled on a cloth, to provide the exceptional gleam to her cherished pieces). There were shelves of books, a couple of brilliantly colourful paintings which he recognised as being by the Irish painter Yeats, whose work Jonathan had discovered while on his fact-finding trip to Ireland, and at the far end of the room, there was a dais on which stood an artist's easel, swathes of fabrics and numerous drawing pads of varying sizes. Obviously Miss O'Carroll worked from home as well as from her exclusive shop.

A little later, the smell of the coffee percolator brought Mrs Nelligan into the lounge followed by Katie with a tray, and as they sat sipping a brew so good that Jonathan was even more determined not to let such a paragon escape him, Mrs Nelligan began to recount the problems mounting up in Hackstown.

'The co-operative idea has possibilities,' said Katie thoughtfully. 'But it will hardly produce all the capital you will need, will it?'

'Dear me no, it will not,' replied her aunt. 'But it will get a commitment from the local population and an involvement. But one of my boys is something on the stock exchange, or in investments or some such job, and I expect to obtain some assistance from him in raising capital.'

'That may prove a little slow for your purposes, Aunt Agnes,' said Katie. 'You do realise that support from that kind of source will mean endless interference from outside investors. Now if you could only come up with a sleeper –'

'A *what*, my dear?' said Mrs Nelligan in some puzzlement.

'A "sleeper" – an "angel", as they call it in the theatre. Someone who would advance the cash and then let you get on with doing the job without wanting to oversee every last move you make. The "angel" puts up the capital and takes a share of the profits and some of the risks but none of the actual operational activity.'

'Not in Ireland, I'm afraid,' said Mrs Nelligan with considerable regret. 'We are going through a recession that is making the Black Forty-Seven look like a Roman Feast. I'm afraid that offshore oil is taking up all the financial slack there is about. The profit returns appear to be less hazardous, I understand, even if they do keep drilling in all the wrong places!'

And it was then that Jonathan gained the undying friendship of Mrs Nelligan and lit a spark of awareness of his talents in the beautiful Katie. He suddenly snapped his fingers.

'I've just had an idea,' he said. 'You ought to come on my dad's TV show and talk about Hickstown.'

'*Hackstown*, dear boy,' corrected Mrs Nelligan gently.

'Sure, Hackstown. It would be a terrific way of contacting your ex-pupils so that you can tell them about the problems. I guess enough of your old boys are running organisations and public companies here which would be well-heeled enough to hand over a stake to build the complex. Then you wouldn't have to worry about interference; America is far enough away to keep folks off your back while you get on with building and running the place. A donation would be a good public relations exercise for most of them anyhow. Hands across the sea and all that.'

'Jonathan, how clever of you!' exclaimed Katie. 'Your dad's show goes out coast to coast and will be seen by just about everyone. And since Aunt Agnes's boys are spread all over the States, it will be a marvellously time-saving method of contacting them. They'll be bound to help out, being Auntie's "old boys".'

Mrs Nelligan smiled happily. 'That would certainly be of considerable assistance to me,' she agreed, patting Jonathan's hand. 'I have some other possible sources to go to as well which I hope to arrange tomorrow. Perhaps it would be possible to meet your father on Monday evening. It would be nice if you could both come to dinner with us.'

She looked questioningly at Katie who nodded in agreement. Anything which would move things along for her beloved Aunt Agnes was all right by her, and it would be exciting to meet Daniel Hogan, who, to be honest, made up in pure showmanship what he may have lacked in intellectualism. Which was not to say that Hogan senior was a Dumkopf. His daily talk show was the longest running of its kind on television and, over the years, anyone who was someone was bound to turn up on *Hogan's Hello* to be introduced to the great American world of screen watchers. And the show ran live without any real format beyond the regular breaks for television advertising which Hogan denigrated to such a degree that there was a queue to buy prime time on his slots, thereby proving his point that the more stick you gave the product, the more the public clamoured to buy it. All of which meant that no one ever quite knew what was gong to happen on the show so audiences watched with compulsive eagerness in the hope that some decent bit of controversy would occur – which it very often did.

Jonathan took a cab home where his parent was viewing

the day's show on video, making notes and mumbling as he did so.

'Today's show was far too lightweight,' he grumbled as Jonathan poured them drinks. 'What I need is something with a bit of serious meat to it and all I get offered is a bunch of damn comics or a clutch of female singers waving their crotches at the cameras and believing that will make up for not having a voice.'

'Well relax, Dad,' Jonathan comforted. 'I've got a real beaut for you – you'll love this one. She's a retired school-teacher from Ireland and you'll never guess what she's about.'

With some detail Jonathan informed his father of his meeting with Mrs Nelligan and all that transpired from it, but he was careful to leave out much reference to her niece – Hogan senior was highly sensitive to his son's romantic attachments, and anyway, he had himself a definite eye for a prettily feathered bird. With his undoubted charm, his air of glamour not to mention the fine head of silver hair which gave him a slightly old-fashioned artistic appearance that seemed to attract even the most sophisticated of women, Jonathan was not taking any chances of being insided by his dad before he got a little closer to Katie.

His dad was delighted – it wasn't difficult to see the kind of attraction such an interview would have for his viewers. Then he had an even better idea.

'Know what I think we should do?' he said, grabbing a notebook and settling into his armchair, obviously pre-pared to start work on a preliminary outline there and then.

'We'll take the interview first, and then open the phone lines to a Pledge Programme – see what kind of dough we bring in by inviting people to telephone in their money pledges while the programme is running and maybe set a preliminary target, like the March of Dimes used to do. I'll guarantee that we'll start something with this one. It could go on for days. We might get a few movie stars to man the telephones so the pledgers get to talk to the stars on air. There are plenty of angles to it, so let's make a few notes, OK?'

Jonathan groaned. 'Dad, I've just flown back from Ireland and I'm bushed. Couldn't we hold on until morning and get the show team working on it first thing?'

Hogan senior shook his head. 'Listen, if you want this item off the ground in a hurry, then we'll have to do the most of the outline on it tonight, else it might be shelved for a week. Now go and make a pot of coffee and we'll get started.'

Two hours later they sat back, contented. They had a working outline they knew would be acceptable to sponsors and producer alike, while the viewers of *Hogan's Hello* would put their dollars where their dialling fingers were, particularly the considerable viewing public with Irish connections, which Daniel Hogan sagely estimated was about eighty per cent of his audience on any given day.

Back at Katie's apartment they were about to hit the sheets, when Katie asked her aunt what her plans were for the morning.

'We could find you some clothes in the shop first thing and then we could do a little sightseeing. Monday morning is usually pretty hectic with me but perhaps we could meet for lunch?'

'Please do not concern yourself with me,' replied Mrs Nelligan. 'I expect to be tied up myself on Monday until the evening. But I would be pleased to renew my wardrobe tomorrow. It will be unusual to have a shop completely to one's self!'

'Where are we planning to go on Monday then? Have you someone you must see?' Katie asked as she reached over to put out the bedside light.

'You could say that, yes. Actually I expect to visit the White House in the afternoon, once I make a telephone call to confirm the appointment.'

Katie sat up, her mouth falling open in some amazement. 'The White House?' she echoed.

'Yes, I expect to visit the President's wife. One of my boys is something rather important there and I will be confirming an appointment I had him make for me before I came to New York. One great thing about America is the convenience with which one can catch an internal flight to almost anywhere,' said Mrs Nelligan with a satisfied air, settling comfortably among the pillows, while her niece extinguished the light without another word.

Five minutes later, Katie sat up in bed again. 'Aunt Agnes, what has the President's wife got to do with you?'

Mrs Nelligan raised her head from her pillow. 'Well,' she said patiently, 'you see, my dear, that parcel of common land I told you about – the one currently in use by the Hackstown Gun Club – actually belongs to your President's wife. One of my boys who is in genealogy recently traced it to her family when I contacted him. Mind you, it goes back quite a bit, but it was never taken over or put to use, so technically, she is now the present owner. I intend to ask her to donate it to build the complex on it. In an election year, it would look so good to the Irish–American voters, don't you think?'

And tucking the blankets in around her shoulders, Mrs Nelligan closed her eyes.

Chapter Five

Mrs Nelligan was abroad bright and early next morning having slept her usual sleep of the righteous, not to say the bold. She pottered about Katie's kitchen, exclaiming over the countless gadgets she found there, and somewhat disconcerted to discover that there was no tea caddy with her favourite morning starter therein.

All she could find was coffee, plus a herbal tea mixture which she did not dare to try. However, just as she was about to settle reluctantly for American coffee, she came across a carton of teabags which, much against her better judgement, she had to make do with. Mrs Nelligan was old-fashioned about her breakfast brew, and in Hackstown the grocer knew better than to offer her the cardboard box with its little white perforated bags when her order list asked for best quality tea. Mrs Nelligan was convinced what was contained in the little sachets was leaf dust, and as such, quite unsuitable for civilised expert tea tasters like herself. And Agnes could speak with some little authority – after all, one of her boys was the son of a wealthy tea planter, being groomed to take over the family business, and he passed on to her what knowledge he gained from his father, on the ins and outs of tea blending, quality and selection.

Taking the first sip of it, she shuddered delicately, and vowed that her first purchase when the markets opened, was going to be a quarter-pound of the best Ceylon she could obtain. Then she poured Katie a cup of coffee and went in with it to her niece.

'Katie my dear,' she said gently, as they sipped companionably together, 'I don't want you to mention to Jonathan's father just yet, about my visit to the White House. I think we should keep that as a little surprise. If it works out as I hope it may, we could tell him all about it on the television show, couldn't we?' She looked guilelessly at her niece, her blue eyes widening in a most innocent fashion.

Katie winked back at her. 'Aunt Agnes, you are a wicked lady!' she told her.

Mrs Nelligan looked shocked. 'Why Katie,' she protested, 'all I am doing is maintaining an element of surprise. I always remember Jeremy Cranfield – one of my boys who later did rather well at writing detective novels – he always said that the success of a story lay in the writer's ability to maintain an element of the unexpected which whetted the reader's appetite. Now we can achieve that for Mr Hogan and his programme if we surprise him as much as we surprise his audience, don't you think?'

As soon as could be considered a decent hour, Mrs Nelligan was on the telephone to her boy in the White House. 'Jimmy' James Stafford had been an obedient ex-pupil. Not only had her appointment with the President's wife been arranged, but the efficient Jimmy had booked her on the most convenient flight to Washington, which would, he explained, get her to the White House in time to join the First Lady in a little luncheon repast, over which they could discuss the matter which had brought Mrs Nelligan to America. Furthermore, Jimmy had also arranged for an official car to pick up Mrs Nelligan at Katie's apartment to ferry her to the airport in comfort and, he advised, he would personally meet the plane in Washington, even if he did have to squeeze in a Presidential briefing beforehand. Jimmy, Katie decided, certainly deserved his job on organisational ability alone.

'Ah yes,' reminisced Mrs Nelligan, 'Jimmy had a passion for organising things when he was at school. We always left him the rosters to see to, and the sports events to organise, as well as any concerts or cultural events. He had a positive genius for having people in the right places when they should be – I wasn't at all surprised when he was offered his present position at the White House. I cannot think of anyone who would organise the President more efficiently than Jimmy.'

'Now Katie,' she advised her niece before she finally left to catch her Washington flight, after an enthralling couple of hours spent choosing her new wardrobe at 'Katinka's'. 'You mustn't worry about the dinner menu for Mr Hogan. I expect to be back from Washington long before you close shop for the day, so I will cook dinner for us. I think we should give the Hogans a good Irish meal. It should make a nice change from hamburgers and lemon meringue pie.' And having ascertained the location of the nearest supermarket to Katie's apartment, Mrs Nelligan took the elevator to the ground floor where a polite and helpful young man was waiting with a departmental limmo at the ready to whisk her on her way to the airport.

It was rather nice being treated like a VIP, Mrs Nelligan reflected as she relaxed in some sophistication in the executive section of the plane, of which she was the only occupant. The stewardess managed to make her a pot of what she termed 'proper tea' and it came with mouth-watering *petit fours*, which, the hostess assured her, were the first choice of the President himself – when he wasn't sucking on his favourite mint humbugs.

'And what is the favourite sweetmeat of the President's wife?' Mrs Nelligan asked eagerly – after all, there were lots of shops in the airport concourse where a potential luncheon guest might add a little dietary something to the gifts already wrapped and packaged ready for presentation at the right moment. Surprisingly, the air hostess sniffed slightly.

'Her ladyship?' she said. 'She never eats a thing that contains flour or sugar – and she'd probably prefer a box of slimming pills to a box of candies any day.'

By which Mrs Nelligan gathered that the First Lady was not the universal American living doll the media cared to make her.

She probed delicately, never actually putting in an indiscreet question – you never discovered who wrote the graffiti on the class blackboard if you asked directly, even if you could literally see the chalk dust on the fingers of the guilty one. And within minutes, she discovered that Herself (as she termed the august First Lady) was highly weight-conscious, fashion-mad, bossy in the extreme, demanding

44

of those who served her, a sucker for good-looking males with a talent for discerning the best flattery button to push at any given moment, and dead ambitious to get her husband back in office – until the political wind of change or a coronary prompted his retirement to the farm in Texas she had made him purchase when the country boy image was popular with his public. Mrs Nelligan learned too that the First Lady was a razor-sharp opportunist, faster at thinking on her feet than her husband would ever be, but sufficiently tunnel-visioned to be a little flattered (though she herself would say 'merely amused') when people were overheard calling her 'Madam President'. On the other hand, she could make quite a good friend – if a bad enemy, was given to sudden gestures of kindliness when her emotions got touched, and had a total blind motherly affection for her sons. With a reputation such as that, Mrs Nelligan calculated, how the power game would come out at the White House was purely academic at any level.

Jimmy, true to his word, was at the airport to meet her, and whirled her away for her appointment. As they drove through without once being halted, Agnes began to feel a little disappointed. No one asked her to open her purse; Jimmy didn't have to mention a special password before they were allowed to approach their destination; even her packages were ignored on the seat beside her. She took Jimmy to task about it. He grinned. 'You've been cleared, Mrs Nelligan – and we *do* take care of our First Family.'

Mrs Nelligan took a final look in her compact mirror to check that her nose wasn't shiny and her lipstick was unsmudged. She was rather pleased with her new outfit, a delicate shell-pink two-piece in fine crêpe with a silk ruffle in a deeper shade of rose-pink down the bodice. Katie had lent her a fur wrap of soft chinchilla and its pearly grey tint was perfect with her silver hair. Agnes *felt* rich and that, she told herself, was more than halfway to appearing to *be* rich. And she had a gut feeling that it might be important.

As she waited for her hostess in the private sitting room to which she had been brought, Mrs Nelligan looked around at its furnishings. Pleasant and quite tasteful, she thought, if you ignored a few aberrations like the odd-looking folded over tricycle wheel with its spokes twisted into convulsive shapes, mounted on top of a concrete block, which had a central position in one window. Modern art, she sniffed to herself, and checking the brass plate beneath it, discovered it to be the product of one of the Family. And then she recalled that the Randolphs' Number Two son was doing his artistic thing in Paris at one of the larger Art schools. Then there were the mock fur throw-overs on the matched settees by the pale-blue painted walls. Real leopardskin, she felt, could only be approved of if the leopard was still wearing it, – and a synthetic copy was innately vulgar, even if it was a First Lady's personal choice.

Then the door opened and Jimmy came in, preceded by the President's wife. Mrs Nelligan's first impression was of a wafer-thin woman of considerable height, with a long face and a rather squarely stubborn jawline, surmounted by an expertly coiffeured head of dark red hair. A pair of piercing blue eyes swept their glance over Agnes, taking in every last seam of her outfit, every shade of her silver hairdo, and giving an immediate approving flicker at the entire effect. She gave Mrs Nelligan a beaming smile which quite transformed her initially plain appearance, and swept forward with hand outstretched.

'Mrs Nelligan – how nice that you could make it to Washington. I hope you had a pleasant flight from New York?'

Jimmy, standing in the background, was entirely ignored and his planned introduction went unused. But then, he was used to being swept aside when the First Lady wanted to make an instant impact, and he couldn't help giving a small internal snigger when he realised that his boss's wife was under the misapprehension that her jolly girls together act was going to deceive Mrs Nelligan. His ex-teacher was even now moving forward with considerable presence to face the First Lady, and then, to Jimmy's infinite surprise, Agnes gave the slightest but most dignified of bows, a quite unmistakable gesture of respect that the First Lady later said was obviously the 'kind of thing done in Irish Royal court circles', which only went to show how well versed she was not, in Irish affairs of a social nature.

46

'Jimmy, pour us both a drink and then you can order lunch,' she said, steering Mrs Nelligan towards one of the leopardskin couches, upon which Agnes seated herself with some revulsion.

Jimmy, remembering quite a long way back, for which he gained Mrs Nelligan's appreciative nod, poured her a pale and extremely dry sherry, and was about to administer the usual small bourbon and water – which was the only alcoholic drink the First Lady allowed herself during the daylight hours – when she frowned at him, and he immediately poured her a glass of the same sherry he had served to Mrs Nelligan.

Luncheon arrived, and while the First Lady dabbled unhappily with two prawns and a strip of lemon peel off a lettuce leaf, Mrs Nelligan got her first taste of American fried chicken, which (she told Katie later) did not impress her in the slightest; she was, she went to some pains to remind her niece, accustomed to free-range fowl, and the tender but tasteless chicken breast served to her was not compensated for by the mouth-watering vegetables that came with it. The french fries she left unexplored, since she believed that a french fry by any other name was still a chip and Mrs Nelligan was totally opposed to what she considered was the total destruction of Ireland's premier vegetable.

'Jimmy, you can get back to your office now,' the First Lady said. 'Mrs Nelligan and I are going to have a little chat on our own.'

'You're sure you don't want me to stay a little longer, ma'am?' Jimmy asked hopefully, for even the efficient James was not entirely privy to Mrs Nelligan's information, and he was understandably anxious to get the inside story before anyone else did.

'No Jimmy, you scat like a good boy!' replied the First Lady dismissively, turning her back so that the luckless Jimmy had no option but to retire and shut the door behind him.

When he had left, the First Lady tiptoed over to the door and then whipped it open. Mrs Nelligan looked slightly disapproving. None of her boys, she told herself, would have demeaned the standards of honour taught to them at her Academy by standing to eavesdrop outside a closed door. That the First Lady should even think of such a heinous failing as being part of the make-up of 'Jimmy' James Stafford gave her yet another insight to the lady's own character. It was, she feared, a case of evil being in the eye of the beholder. Eavesdropping for the acquisition of valuable information was just the sort of uncivilised activity people in Irish political life took as an essential fixture in their race for slices of the political pie, and there was no reason to suppose that American power play was conducted by any different rules. Her Jimmy, she reasoned, was not really a political animal – he was a Public Relations organiser – and if his abilities had taken him into the world of government, she was sure his indoctrination in the tenets of good behaviour, honour, trust, truth, conscience and self-sacrifice was firmly established, having been firmly nurtured by herself in his youth. Or at least she hoped so. As she watched Jimmy's tall mohair-suited figure stride quickly down the corridor outside, she preferred to believe that her trust in his behavioural standards was still unsullied.

'They all hang around hoping to catch an earful of something they shouldn't,' confided the First Lady as she resumed her seat beside Mrs Nelligan. 'You can't trust a damn one of them.'

'It was most kind of you to see me at such short notice,' said Mrs Nelligan sipping her second pale sherry with an appreciation not quite shared by the President's Lady who actually couldn't stand sherry because it gave her a headache.

'Nonsense,' said the First Lady. 'When Jimmy told me all about you, I knew we couldn't let you leave the States without making your acquaintance. Anyway, you probably know we have a great interest in the Irish in America – where would the Republican Party be without the Irish?'

'Or indeed, the Democrats?' said Mrs Nelligan, putting down her sherry on the small inlaid table beside her.

'Of course,' said the First Lady without a great deal of enthusiasm as she thought of all the wasted votes that

Irish–American allegiance to the Opposition totalled up. It had been a situation of the deepest regret to her that her husband's roots were firmly and inextricably placed in the deepest of British soil and his hopes of obtaining the Irish–American vote at election time were not going to be realised by announcements that his ancestors came over on the *Mayflower*, what with the Irish race memory being what it is. Worse still, according to his advisors, was the historical fact that a relative on his father's side was known to have had a job with the immigration authorities on Ellis Island in the 1800s – and that was practically yesterday, as far as the Irish with family histories of coffin ships were concerned. So all in all, her husband couldn't bank on sentiment to give him a Gaelic voting landslide. She sighed slightly. There were times when she wished she'd settled for a husband in the real estate business.

'What an attractive room,' said Mrs Nelligan politely, carefully avoiding any concentration of gaze on the tricycle wheel sculpture at the window, and fastening her eye instead on a somewhat amateurish painting hanging on the opposite wall.

'You collect paintings?' she enquired. 'I cannot say the artist of that particular style is one I am familiar with. I expect it may be one of your American Impressionist painters?' She sent a quick plea to the Creator for forgiveness, since the painting in question was of a somewhat block-legged little girl of about nine, standing in what she hoped was a cornfield, unless by now the Yanks had discovered a method of growing macaroni sticks, with an orange sun overhead, and a trio of unlikely looking birds of indeterminate breed flying backwards into a tree – that is if you accepted the angle of their wings as being correct.

The First Lady was enchanted. 'My, do you think it good?' she trilled. 'Actually, the President painted that picture himself when we were on holiday at our farm in Texas. Of course, he had to imagine the little girl, but I think he got the cornfield pretty good. He finds painting a great relaxation – just like your statesman Winston Churchill did.'

Mrs Nelligan closed her eyes momentarily. 'Your

husband seems to have quite – surprising – talent,' she said politely, ignoring the Churchillian reference which at this stage was too complicated to try and sort out.

'I must tell you, I *love* your outfit,' said the First Lady, determined to return a compliment. 'It's just the prettiest colour and I adore the cut.'

Mrs Nelligan smiled. 'The best of Irish and American fashion, I hope,' she said easily. 'I got it in New York but the designer is Irish.'

She reached over and produced her gifts handing them to the First Lady. 'I hope you will like these little gifts from one of our Irish craft producers. No two are alike; the colours for each garment are specially dyed by hand, so that each is unique.'

It says much for the self-discipline of such a totally dedicated follower of fashion like the F.L. that she managed to refrain from ripping off the wrappings to see what lay inside the boxes until after Mrs Nelligan had left to return to New York. Then she was ecstatic to discover a gilet of finest shadow tweed with a matched skirt and a co-related fine woven shadow tweed shawl – for which, when she wore it, she gained a valuable political edge for her husband, when the Primaries began later the following year in the American–Irish areas.

It was while they were sipping coffee that Mrs Nelligan finally broached the subject which had taken her to Washington.

'Mrs Randolph, have you ever investigated your own antecedents?' she began gently.

The First Lady looked puzzled. 'My family were all from New England, and I understand that my great-great-grandfather and his six brothers came to America via the West Indies, though no one seems to be quite sure just what they were all doing out there. I think the family must have been a sea-going one, that went out from either England or Scotland. It wasn't that important to us when I was a little girl and there never seemed to be the need to check any further back than my great-grandparents in New England, once I grew up.'

'Ah,' said Mrs Nelligan with some pleasure, for like the

50

rest of us, she also enjoyed being the bearer of interesting tidings. 'I have a further gift for you. Your complete family tree right back as far as records go – and in fact to an early king of the Irish province of Leinster up in the County Meath. You may know that Meath is the ancient site of the headquarters of the Royal Houses of Ireland – you have no doubt heard of Tara?'

Breathlessly, the First Lady nodded (she too had wept over *Gone with the Wind* and the name was quite familiar, even if she had the association quite incorrect.)

Mrs Nelligan unfolded an imposing looking parchment which the obedient Pidgie had had illustrated in easy-to-read colours that gave in impressive detail the roots of the President's Lady, tracing her family all the way back through a couple of renegades, one pirate (hanged in Jamaica), a highwayman, a couple of foot-soldiers, several sailors, a serving maid with whom, unfortunately, a young master had evidently exercised his droit de seigneur with obvious results which were, it would seem, carefully dispatched to Australia in the mid-eighties, and several virtuous housewives, married into highly respected households, whose capacity to produce large numbers of offspring kept the name of the family in church records of one kind or another. The exciting bit was the direct lineage to an early owner of Courtfield Abbey which had been plundered from a community of monks, donated by a Norman overlord to the First Lady's forebears for favours rendered, and held in a loose sort of fashion until the family left for England in 1847 when the famine hit Ireland.

The First Lady was incredulous. To her credit she was already calculating the value of the revelations to her husband when he had another go at becoming the President of America for a second term. Later the obvious cache to her own standing would hit her.

'My family really can trace back its origins to a Gaelic king?' she exclaimed.

'The authenticity is quite beyond question,' replied Mrs Nelligan firmly. 'One of my past pupils happens to be the leading expert on genealogy in Ireland – in fact, he holds the chair at one of our Irish universities. He traced your family back and had this chart drawn up for me to bring to you.'

The First Lady sat up a little straighter, gazing dreamily out of the window. 'My husband will certainly be pleased. It will make quite a difference when the Primaries come up,' she told Mrs Nelligan. 'You know, all this has quite made my day!'

Mrs Nelligan smiled. 'I am so glad you are pleased. The Irish connection with my own village of Hackstown is of particular importance, of course. Courtfield Castle is one of the ancient ruins in the locality, and indeed a major landmark in the district. It had quite a landholding with it when it was occupied by your ancestors.'

Again the First Lady thought of the romance of having a family who were major landowners. It made the thirty-acre farm in New England on which she grew up with few conveniences and no luxuries, suddenly seem a little more bearable for the first time since she had cut and run to work as a clerk at one of the government departments in Washington, where she had finally met, and manipulated up the aisle of the local Baptist chuch, the young senator from Indiana whom she later accompanied to the White House. Mrs Nelligan fed her fishing line out a little more.

'The title of course, passed through the eldest male of your family but the original last will and testament of the last occupant of the Abbey was somewhat unusual, my ex-pupil told me. It stated that the lands of the Hillside and environs of Moane, were to be bequeathed in perpetuity to the descendants of your family, again through the eldest member, but it did not state that the member had to be of the male sex. Now as I understand it, you were the only child of your parents, and therefore, naturally, the eldest. Thus, it would seem that the lands are, technically speaking, yours.'

Mrs Nelligan sat back, observing with considerable contentment the effect of her words on America's First Lady.

'How much of an area are we talking about?' the First Lady asked in hushed tones.

'Around a hundred and fifty acres give or take a few,' said Mrs Nelligan easily.

'I guess it's all unusable bogland?' asked the F.L. with

small hope of being proven mistaken.

'Well,' said Mrs Nelligan judiciously, 'there is a fair share of bog, scrub and rough terrain, a good trout lake, a woodland area and hilly land of course – but it has some commercial value. At present it is being used by the local Gun Club as a shooting preserve. They have held the land as a private reserve for quite a number of years.'

The First Lady looked disappointed.

'But it is yours by right, you know,' said Mrs Nelligan, 'and you can do with it what you wish.'

The First Lady looked more cheerful. 'Well, of course, I wouldn't want to upset anyone. After all it is really only a nominal sort of thing, isn't it?' she asked.

'On the contrary,' said Mrs Nelligan. 'Your landholding is of major importance to Hackstown at this moment in time.'

'It is?' asked the First Lady.

'Definitely.'

Mrs Nelligan settled back into the leopardskin throw-over which was proving surprisingly cosy.

'Hackstown,' she began, 'has fallen on somewhat difficult commercial times. In short, the only factory in the village – which, I must add, was American financed – was for years the main source of employment for the majority of the local workforce. It is being put into receivership very shortly. This will leave Hackstown without any commercial income, either coming into the stores in the village, or into the pockets of the residents.' She gazed earnestly at the First Lady. 'This, you will understand, Mrs Randolph, is not exactly to the advantage of anyone in Hackstown. Indeed the entire welfare of the district has hinged upon the progress made by your countrymen in their factory in Hackstown.'

The First Lady looked suitably concerned, though she was wondering just where all this was leading to, and exactly what it all had to do with her family being Irish landowners and the descendants of King Illan of Leinster.

Mrs Nelligan now proceeded to illuminate the situation. 'We can make excellent use of that tract of land which belongs to your family if we are given proper legal title to it. I believe it would convert into an excellent tourist complex

53

designed on Celtic mythological lines and this would bring employment to Hackstown on a permanent basis, and thus save my village from what can only be described as total disintegration.'

She proceeded to explain the concept of the Tir na n-Og project, producing rabbit-like from her handbag a most artistically designed sketch plan of how she envisaged the finished complex.

The First Lady grasped the potential in a trice – in fact, overall, she was a jump ahead of Mrs Nelligan.

'You'd certainly pull in the American tourists with this idea, and once they realised it was a donation from the Presidential family, they would be even more interested. And of course, it could do nothing but good all around, particularly next year,' she commented.

Then Mrs Nelligan, scenting victory, got her brightest idea of the day.

'That castle ruin on the map,' she pointed. 'Now that could be renamed Illan Castle, after your ancestor, and perhaps one room rebuilt and furnished as an ancient Irish banquet hall just as it must have been when King Illan lived. We already have several of these old castles running tourist banquets during the summer season and they seem to be most popular with visitors.'

The First Lady was enchanted with the idea and had a couple of suggestions of her own to make.

'My son, who is studying Art in Paris, France, would be most useful to you, Mrs Nelligan. I am sure he would be happy to design you something marvellous if you want statues or monuments to decorate the place. He's going to be the leading American sculptor when he finishes his course.'

Mrs Nelligan swallowed slightly but gave a non-committal murmur, vowing in her heart not to let young Alvin Randolph within the proverbial ass's-roar of the artistic furnishings for the complex, if his tricycle wheel was any indication of the breadth of his talent. Macaroni-stick cornfields she could bury as folk art on the complex walls, but bent wheels would be impossible to explain away even to Americans.

'There is only one problem,' said Mrs Nelligan as she folded away the illustrations and maps. 'The local Gun Club have what they regard as a divine right to shoot over your land and they will be loath to give up that privilege without a struggle.'

The First Lady's lip went out aggressively.

'It's my land, and if I wanna do something with it, then as you say, it's my right,' she said firmly.

Mrs Nelligan nodded with one of her childlike fluttering glances into the First Lady's face.

'But of course,' she said, 'you know that and I know that – but then we both know what men are like. They stick together, and when they get an idea into their heads, it is very difficult to disabuse them of it. Now the Gun Club committee believes that Hackstown needs a Gun Club before it needs jobs, largely because its select body of members are of ample financial means, and they are quite sure they will retain the land in question.'

The First Lady got up from the settee. 'We'll see about that,' she said, and rang a buzzer at a desk just inside the door. Almost immediately the door opened and 'Jimmy' James Stafford came in.

'Ma'am?' he asked, and the First Lady glowered at him. 'Don't tell me you don't know what this is all about. You've been stashed outside there for a good hour, so I guess there's little about this you haven't overheard,' she said.

Jimmy blushed, sliding a quick look at his ex-headmistress.

'Well, I couldn't help overhearing the odd word, ma'am,' he excused himself. 'But what is it you want me to do for you?'

'Just check I can accept this, and then do as I wish with the deeds, on a personal basis of course. We don't want any complications for the President, do we?'

Mrs Nelligan realised with some relief that it would not be advisable to offer a percentage of the potential profit from the complex to the owner of the land. However, she made a mental note to do the decent thing and find a charity which the First Lady would be interested in supporting and see that a regular donation was made with due ceremony, and devoutly she prayed it would be something innocuous like a bird sanctuary, and not the Friendly Sons of St Patrick or Noraid.

Chapter Six

In no time flat, 'Jimmy' James was back with the good news:
the First Lady could avail herself of her inheritance and
hand it over to whomsoever she wished, just as long as she
wasn't thinking of making a profit out of the transaction –
like taking a lump sum or negotiating a yearly cheque. Not
that it would be illegal, merely highly unpolitical, seeing as
how during election times just about everyone in the US
government was likely to be investigated for all forms of tax
evasion, graft, bribes, donations to the Party, and gifts
which exceeded the official financial limits, or any other
freebee on offer.

'Let's make a formal occasion out of it when you hand
over the deeds to Mrs Nelligan,' suggested Jimmy with an
over-eager eye on the Public Relations potential.

Mrs Nelligan meantime, was explaining sweetly to the
First Lady about her intended appearance on *Hogan's
Hello* and her hopes to raise the necessary capital to put the
complex into construction – all of which, being a practical
businesswoman, the First Lady quite understood and
appreciated.

She took a straight look at Mrs Nelligan and said, 'I know
exactly what you have in mind. You're going to land it on
him on the programme about this tract belonging to me,
aren't you?'

Mrs Nelligan blushed slightly. 'Do you mind? I did intend
to ask your permission of course. It seems an ideal occasion
to do so and it could raise so much interest in the project.'

The First Lady laughed. 'Of course you should do so.
You'd be crazy to pass up such a chance. It's exactly what I'd
do myself, and between the two of us, I look forward to
seeing you catch Daniel Hogan on the hop. He's quite a guy,

but I owe him a couple because he's not always the kindest to my husband, and he's been quite uncomplimentary about my Alvin's sculpture.'

Mrs Nelligan suddenly began to feel a glimmering of affection for Hogan senior; anyone with that much taste and the courage to admit it, was on the up and up in her book. A couple of smaller convolutions in barbed wire which the proud First Lady had wheeled in to show off as a further sample of the still undiscovered genius of her Number Two son, had now convinced Agnes that if she didn't get the hell out and back to New York, she would run out of artistically flavoured platitudes and be obliged to let her natural excellent taste spoil the whole thing.

Deciding she could safely leave the official hand-over arrangements to the efficient 'Jimmy' James to organise, she limousined it back to Dulles airport in good time to make her afternoon flight back to New York, and her dinner preparations.

Finding the cooking wherewithal in her niece's kitchen presented certain difficulties. Katie ran a great freezer stock but not a great deal in actual dry ingredients. It took a couple of trips to the local supermarket before Agnes put together all she needed to make up her Irish-oriented dinner menu. Fortunately, as she told Katie later, she met up with a very helpful young woman behind the meat counter, who, being a native of Dublin's Liberties area, and only five years over in what she was pleased to continually call The Big Apple, had not forgotten her roots so completely as not to recognise the makings of a decent Irish culinary masterpiece when she was asked for them.

Katie returned from work to an apartment redolent of the most enticing cooking odours (in fact, she never again had quite the same appreciation for TV dinners once her Aunt Agnes returned to Ireland and home cooking was no longer part of her diet). She poured her aunt a pre-guest-arrival sherry, while Agnes recounted the day's adventures.

'You know that "Jimmy" James Stafford will make a total meal out of this,' Katie reminded her. 'He's very Public Relations minded, particularly when it can do some good among the districts where the Party needs a bit of propping up.'

'But of course,' said Mrs Nelligan smiling gently. 'Jimmy will make a delightful occasion out of the event. He will organise everything to perfection and with the best of good taste. It will help the voting for Horace Randolph and the promotion of the new complex for Hackstown. People will want to come and see it when we have it completed, so Jimmy will help the tourist influx to us with this little ceremony. And anyway, he does love arranging gatherings ...'

'Have you any idea what he has in mind and when he plans to hold his little shindig?' her niece asked.

Mrs Nelligan shook her head. 'I believe they are going to move the official schedule around a little so that the presentation of the deeds should happen within a week. I expect it will be held in Washington, so I will probably fly up there again – really, it is all quite tiring at my age!'

Katie chuckled. 'From what I have seen of you at your age in the past twenty-four hours, you're about as fragile as the Statue of Liberty, Aunt Agnes.'

Mrs Nelligan opened her blue eyes innocently at her niece.

'I believe the occasion will be informal – you know, cocktails after six, friends of the Randolphs and the immediate family, a few executives from the White House of course and, naturally, selected people from the media, Jimmy told me as he took me to the airport today. He hasn't worked it all out yet, but he will be contacting me in a couple of days.'

The door buzzer went and Katie went to open it, while her aunt took a last look at the perfectly cooked meal she had warming on the hostess trolley. It was a meal fit for even a President's Lady. Mrs Nelligan, among her other talents, was a cook with inspiration and a discoverer over the years of regional dishes which were long forgotten by modern culinary experts of her acquaintance. So, for the occasion, Agnes had dug deep into her memory and produced a poached Irish salmon (at least her friend in the supermarket assured her the fish came from Ireland) with a dressing not to be found in any printed cookbook since, years ago, Agnes had taken it down in writing from an eighty-year-old ex-housekeeper at one of Co. Galway's Great Houses. She was to follow this with a special casserole of beef which was cooked to a local Hackstown recipe that required a marinade of Irish Guinness, mustard, herbs and spices, and in the fridge, waiting to top off the meal, was a cream mousse which had the tantalising flavour of Irish whiskey.

Agnes had even found time to cook up a feather-light Irish apple cake to go with the coffee she decided to leave to Katie to brew, since good coffee was not her own strong point. For herself, she had run a decent blend of tea to earth and was looking forward to a good strong pot of it after they had demolished the dinner.

Daniel and Jonathan came into the lounge, suddenly filling what had seemed to be a sizeable room. Both father and son were over the six-foot mark and there was an extraordinary likeness between them. Mrs Nelligan could quite clearly see just how Jonathan would look when he reached his father's age. Distinguished, she told herself, wasn't the half of it. Hogan senior had the cheekbones of a James Mason, the brown eyes of a Sharif, the elegantly silvered hair of a Stewart Granger, and when he greeted her, the surprisingly softly modulated voice that she believed only the best psychologist might have. It invited confidences, hinted that it could never be unkind, and suggested infinite understanding. It was perfect for a chat show host, and it was only when the interviewee got comfortable that Daniel Hogan could put a whiplash into his vocal quality that left the subject wide open to the injudicious replies that kept the show in the number one slot week after week.

Daniel Hogan held her hand a little longer than necessary, after Jonathan had made the introductions. Agnes looked back at him, her blue eyes widening and her lashes fluttering in their usual scared robin fashion. Then Daniel Hogan stared straight at the soft pink mouth, seeing in a second the firm decisive lines in the corners of her lips and he winked. From then on, they were allies.

Mrs Nelligan's dinner was a marked success. Jonathan

and his father were not only complimentary to the point of wild enthusiasm, but they cleared their plates and came up for seconds.

'Now I know why every American with any Irish blood in his veins wants to get back to Ireland,' sighed Daniel, as he sipped his second cup of coffee and settled back in Katie's comfortable armchair. 'It's not the leprechauns, it's the cooking.'

Mrs Nelligan blushed. 'A mere trifle, dear Mr Hogan. I am so pleased you enjoyed the meal.'

'Eating out will never be the same again,' said Daniel gallantly, as, with considerable effort, Jonathan eased himself from the couch, and gathered the plates together, preparatory to doing the washing up, like the well-trained diner-à-deux he was.

'Please don't bother,' protested Katie a little half-heartedly since, career girl though she might be, her greatest aversion on the domestic front was having to deal with the washing up.

'Nonsense,' said her aunt handing a couple of knives to her and rapidly gathering the empty vegetable dishes into a tidy pile for Jonathan to remove. 'With both of you manning the sink, the dishes will get done in half the time and it will save both of us in the morning rush tomorrow.' With professional expertise, she manipulated both of them towards the kitchen area and then sat back with a soupçon of cognac to talk to Hogan senior.

It took Katie and Jonathan an hour to clear away the dinner-ware, even with help from Katie's neat little dishwasher. Still, Katie happened to have a bottle of rather well-matured Scotch in her kitchen cupboard and Jonathan was such a good listener when she told him about her commercial enterprises and her high hopes for the future, and of course it was only courteous of her to listen to his life story in return. All in all they found themselves in agreement about a lot of things – motivation, freedom to do one's own thing, abhorrence of hot-dogs with brown sauce, a fondness for reggae music, old movies, and the ideal household pet as being feline. On the other hand they disagreed violently about TV blockbusters, the ideal place to live, colour schemes, women's rights, working wives. But nothing major.

Meantime, Mrs Nelligan had utilised the time by getting acquainted with the mechanics of her television début. Daniel found her delightful – co-operative, unruffled by questions, and with a sly sense of humour which at times convulsed him. He explained how he saw her appearance on the show and the potential of what he was already calling the Investathon. And Daniel had been thinking since he and Jonathan had roughed out their ideas. He had come up with a new variation on their original plan of a phone-in dollars-pledging system. For as little as a two-dollar pledge, the investing public would be eligible to take part in a monster raffle on the show, which would give the winner a free holiday at the Hackstown Tir na n-Og holiday complex, when it was built. Daniel was even planning on inviting one of Hollywood's major movie stars with strong Irish roots to do the draw on the show. Mrs Nelligan fluttered appreciatively, her practical mind already a couple of jumps ahead of Mr Hogan senior. She felt sure she could come up with a rather better personality than a Hollywood star, but that she was going to keep it to herself for a while yet. Daniel was growing more enthusiastic, not to say inspired, by the minute. He was making copious notes about majorettes dressed in Kelly green with harps and shamrocks and shillelaghs, Irish pipers to usher in the huge drum he was planning to use for the draw, and much as Mrs Nelligan detested the idea, she could nevertheless see the merit of the spectacle. She only hoped that the great Irish-American public would see it all as a St Patrick's Day-style romp and accept the schmaltz of it with some good nature.

It was all a far cry from her original discreet hope of contacting her ex-boys for financial assistance. However, she realised its ultimate strength lay in the massive publicity the project would gain, publicity too vast to be ignored by the Hackstown Gun Club committee who would hardly be in a position to vote down the contributions of a million or more Irish–Americans prepared to put their money where their patriotism was. And the more the details were ironed out, the less guilty Agnes was beginning to feel about not telling Daniel in advance about the ownership of the tract of land earmarked for Tir na n-Og. Indeed, she felt that she was helping to bring considerable excitement to the show, and even Daniel himself, she was convinced, would be happier if he were to be surprised 'live' than having to simulate his amazement on camera. It meant, of course, that at some stage she would throw the show into some disruption since she would be disregarding the list of set questions they were going to use to key Daniel's interview. Not that Mrs Nelligan had need of such a prop. As she reminded Daniel, twenty years of unscripted teaching didn't exactly leave one tongue-tied in any situation and anyhow, she would not be able to read a word without her spectacles which she had no intention of wearing on a public television show. Agnes was not without her human frailties, a slight touch of the vanities being one.

'Don't worry about a thing,' said Daniel consolingly. 'I have no doubt but that you will do it perfectly your own way.'

'You can bet on that,' said Katie under her breath, as she and Jonathan resumed their seats, this time sitting noticeably much closer together than they had before dinner.

'Have you ever appeared on television?' Jonathan asked Mrs Nelligan, taking a satisfied sip from a Gaelic coffee which had appeared almost magically in front of him, as Agnes trotted back from the kitchen with the cream-collared steaming glasses, and resumed her seat beside his father.

'Not on an actual programme, you understand, but when I was teaching, we ran a communications course for the senior boys and we set up a studio within the school where they could learn the mechanics. So they used me as a regular interviewee on a variety of subjects,' replied Agnes. 'Actually, it proved a very positive course; one of the boys is now something quite important in television on the West Coast ...' She addressed her last remark to Daniel who nodded politely. 'Ambrose Carter was quite the best of all the seniors who took the course. But then he was always curious about everyone's affairs. I felt he chose the right

63

profession when he went into television, even if his family already had interests in the business.'

And Daniel, realising with some respect just who Mrs Nelligan was actually referring to, began to be convinced that this little old lady was not of the lavender and lace variety but more of the spice and steel. Anyone who could classify the most powerful wheel in West Coast television circles as being a nosey young lad, had to have something going for her!

It was late when the Hogans finally said good night and left, arranging with Katie to bring her aunt to the studios in time for make-up and a pre-show directive. Katie was already mentally surveying her boutique stock to decide what Agnes would wear; a soft lavender crêpe with a touch of violet would look great with Mrs Nelligan's silvery curls and pink complexion, she felt, and there was just the job hanging on the rails among the designer labels she had put away for some of her more favoured clients.

They sat over a last cup of tea when their guests had departed.

'I think it is all going to be very successful,' said Mrs Nelligan. Katie nodded. Then she blushed slightly.

'Aunt Agnes, I have to tell you I mentioned the ownership of that land to Jonathan. It kind of – slipped out – because I – well – thought I should just tell him in passing ... but he has promised he won't say a word to his father about it. As a matter of fact he agreed with you on the surprise element.'

Agnes looked at her niece and smiled gently. 'Of course you did, my dear. I rather thought you might. But I am sure Jonathan has as acute a sense of good television as his father ... such a charming pair, don't you think? That young man has excellent potential – which is one thing I have always recognised in my boys.'

'Do you really think so?' Katie said eagerly, and then as she looked at her aunt, smiling quietly, she began to laugh. 'You,' she said, kissing Agnes on the cheek, 'are a naughty old matchmaker. Don't you know we don't have such things in America?'

Agnes nodded. 'A little help in an hour of need never goes amiss – and I am quite sure you are quite mistaken about my matchmaking. I would never interfere,' and her blue eyes widened innocently as she looked back at her niece.

'You know,' she continued a moment later, 'my missing my original flight has turned out to be quite providential. If I had gone on the earlier plane, I would not have met Jonathan and all this help over the leisure complex might never have happened. I must remember to write and thank the Irish airlines for their courtesy and assistance when this television business is completed.'

Katie thoroughly agreed with her. Fate, she told herself, as she snuggled down under her duvet a little later and put out the light, had a strange way of making life very interesting for unattached young women. And how glad she was at this very minute that she was the young woman in question, and unattached as well!

And Jonathan, when he went to bed at last, dreamed of firm-minded females with hair the colour of autumn leaves, almond-shaped green eyes and a figure it would take a poet to describe adequately. In his dreams he was about to kiss the goddess when she rounded on him and thumped him with a roll of Irish tweed which suddenly opened out and enveloped him. All of which would have meant something to any psychiatrist who might have been asked to interpret the Hogan hallucinations!

Chapter Seven

By six o'clock on the evening of the television show, Agnes
had developed a slight migraine. It wasn't that she was
suffering from pre-show nerves, but rather that everyone
else seemed to be, which gave her a nervous headache.
Trendy young men clad in leather gilets and lumberjack
shirts, or wearing tight suede trousers, topped by silky polo-
necked sweatshirts, and sporting identity bracelets, neck
amulets and Indian copper medallions depending on what
theme in sartorial splendour was being aired and by whom,
were galloping around the studio corridors at a fast lick.
Efficient young women with clipboards, neck timepieces,
large brightly coloured frame spectacles and Bjorn Borg
sweatbands, seemed to be everywhere, ferrying confused-
looking performers from one dressing room to another,
from make-up to studio. In one of her own journeys, Agnes
caught a quick glimpse through an open doorway of what
she took to be a tea urn surrounded by coffee cups, until she
realised that the only liquid likely to be available was the
strong black coffee beloved by the entire American nation.
During another journey, she observed a vision which, she
devoutly prayed, Providence would never repeat as a part of
her life experience. Seated at a table, noisily sucking an
enormous ice-cream soda through a scarlet straw, was a
small boy of about, she estimated, eight years of age,
guarded by an enormously fat woman clad in a Mumu
which ineffectively tried to cover her poundage in a riot of
orange and black patterned nylon satin. She was eating a
cream bun, somewhat messily, running what appeared to be
an admonitory dissertation through the crumbs. The small
boy took his mouth away from the straw and stuck out a
mutinous lower lip.

'But I don' wanna go 'round an' kiss any rotten ladies!' he protested.

'Dwane! Will ya lissen to me? You're supposed to look as cute as a bug – now will ya also act like one and do what Momma tells ya?'

'I don' wanna!'

'Well, that don' matter a whole lot – ya gotta do like I say. You have the Finals in Chicago next week – don' ya wanna make a good impression on the judges who'll be voting there? They'll probably be viewing *Hogan's Hello* so they'll get a chance to see ya before the final. Ya have one up on the rest of the competitors, Dwane honey. Now be a good boy and do like I say.'

The small boy lowered his head and resumed his battle to get the last of the ice-cream soda up through the straw while his mother slurped at her coffee.

She caught sight of Mrs Nelligan and waved in a friendly fashion.

'You appearing on the Hogan show too?' she enquired. Mrs Nelligan nodded. 'How de do? My name is Beth Ann Shreiner and this is my son Dwane. Dwane, say hello to the lady.'

Dwane raised his chin, removed the last vestiges of the soda with a loud *swush*, and scowled at Mrs Nelligan.

Agnes stared straight at him and then gave him her frostiest smile. 'You need not rise, young man. How do you do?' she said quietly, and something in her tone made Dwane's mother give her offspring a quick jab in the rib, so that he reluctantly got up and then actually pulled out the remaining chair for Mrs Nelligan. Even his mother looked surprised.

Mrs Nelligan sat down and regarded the pair with some curiosity. Dwane was already made up with plenty of eye shadow of silvery blue, a deep pink lipstick over which had been put a shiny lip-gloss so that he looked as if he had just emerged from a honey jar. His light blond hair obviously owed a debt to a professional hair-colouring artist (in fact had Agnes been familiar with one of the commercials on *Hogan's Hello* she would have recognised the shade of Dwane's locks as being the one marketed as 'Morning

Fair'). It was tortured into a coiffure of deep corrugated waves that rippled down to the collar of his royal blue velvet suit. The suit jacket was a masterpiece of extravagant bad taste – it had an overcheck of glittering lurex threads while the lapels were covered in white nylon fur – and the trousers were tight to the knee and then widely flared with a narrow matching cuff of white fur. Beneath the jacket, Dwane was wearing a white and gold lace shirt with a gold lurex bow-tie at the neck. His mother kept brushing invisible flecks off the shoulders of his jacket and twitching the bow-tie into place, since every time Dwane moved, it shifted to left off-centre. Agnes, with horror, suddenly observed that his nails were varnished a pale shell pink, and he was actually wearing a blue stone pinkie ring and a chain bracelet with a gilt miniature lock fastening on his wrist.

'My Dwane is appearing too,' explained Mrs Shreiner. 'He's been on most of the networks one way or another ever since he was five. *Hogan's Hello* is the real top of the pile – it will do him a lotta good in Chicago.' She sat back complacently. In spite of herself, Mrs Nelligan's curiosity got the better of her.

'Your son –' she probed delicately – 'Which branch of the theatrical profession is he concentrating on?'

Beth Anne shrieked with delight. 'There Dwane. I told you – that outfit separates ya from the amateurs! This lady recognises a real professional when she sees one!'

Mrs Nelligan closed her eyes for a moment, but since disapproval never gained information, she smiled at Dwane's mother and raised her eyebrows.

'Well,' said Mrs Shreiner, 'Dwane sings, and dances, and he does impressions of Liberace on a little white piano. He's the winner of the semi-final for the "Junior America Talent and Charm" contest which has been running in New York. Next week we go to Chicago for the finals.'

'Really?' said Mrs Nelligan in utter disbelief. 'Your son competes in beauty contests? And what kind of rewards does he obtain?'

'Well,' said Mrs Shreiner reflectively. 'He's won a lotta goods. Dwane's a very successful competitor – real talented and cute as a bug. Judges love him, especially the older

68

female judges.' She smiled fondly at her son, now occupied with shredding all the used plastic cups and drinking straws he could find. 'Of course, he's won some cash too, but that goes on costs. His travel expenses to competition locations are quite unbelievable. His Poppa has to subsidise that – we're divorced, but it comes under Educational Purposes, in the alimony.' She smiled widely and flicked another trace of invisible dust from Dwane's jacket.

'And school?' asked Mrs Nelligan. Mrs Shreiner frowned. 'I hadda get him a private tutor. He didn't like the school back home in Detroit, because the kids were so jealous of him that they gave him a bad time.'

'I can imagine,' said Mrs Nelligan.

'You know,' continued Beth Ann dreamily, 'all my life, I wanted to get into the movies. I took acting lessons when I was seventeen and I actually took a Greyhound to Hollywood. Then I met Dwane's poppa – he was the bus driver. I never did get to Hollywood. We got married in Reno and I ended up keeping house for a guy who was never at home. So I was determined that Dwane would get his chance. I think he's gonna be the male equivalent to Shirley Temple. Any day now I bet we'll get a good TV offer for him for a series and then we're in the Big Time.'

Mrs Nelligan was almost sorry for Beth Ann Shreiner, until she took another look at Dwane, who was now surveying himself in his mother's compact mirror.

'Momma, my chin's beginnin' to shine up again and that dame up in make-up put black instead of brown on my lashes,' he said complainingly. 'C'mon, you gotta tell her so that she'll change it. I don't look good with black mascara – you always say so.'

Immediately, Mrs Shreiner hauled herself to her feet. Her anxiety was patent.

'Dwane honey, I'm sorry. I never noticed what she was doing. Let's go right back and have it all done again. OK?'

She smiled again at Mrs Nelligan. 'Well, see you on the set.' She held out a plump beringed hand. 'Break a leg!'

Agnes looked puzzled and Beth Ann laughed again. 'It's a way of wishing ya luck,' she said as she turned away, followed by a sulky Dwane. As he passed Mrs Nelligan's chair, he kicked at her shin, but quick as he was, Mrs Nelligan beat him to it as she immediately stuck out her other foot and neatly tripped him. He shot forward into his mother's rear, where, fortunately, her bulk was sufficient to prevent him from falling flat on his face. Mrs Nelligan looked calmly at him as he regained his balance. 'You hurt yourself, I trust?' she murmured as she carefully retrieved his gold bow-tie from beneath her chair and returned it to him while his mother collected the contents of her purse from the floor where they had been scattered in the collision.

Dwane blinked, and then, for a moment, turned on his most practised smile which Agnes observed without any change of expression.

'Don't bother, young man,' she said softly. 'I've eaten small boys like you for breakfast back home.' And she patted his velvet-coloured shoulder, managing at the same time to press an experienced finger on a nerve point learned from one of her boys whose sporting interests were served in the martial arts field.

Dwane jumped suddenly, and then he turned to her with a truly boyish grin of respect. 'I like you, lady!' he opined and then was gone in the wake of his mother.

Agnes herself had had a short session with the make-up department whose experts, once they saw her rosy complexion, did no more than flick a peachy powder on her cheeks and emphasise her blue eyes with a touch of shadow. The soft pink lipstick which Katie decided was the correct match for her dress, they left alone, admittedly under some protest since they were into the plummy colours of the current fashion season, and these Mrs Nelligan flatly refused to consider.

'I have no desire to emerge looking like Dracula's mother,' she told the girl firmly. 'I'm quite unconcerned that my lip colour will not thrill your sponsors. And I cannot agree that a set of false eyelashes will make me look "cute" as you are pleased to term it. I am not cute. I never have been cute, even as a little girl, and furthermore, I have no wish to seem cute as an adult.'

And she sailed regally out of the make-up department,

back to her dressing room which was now occupied by an extremely tall woman with a false hair-piece pinned coronet fashion on top of her head, who wore what seemed to be a collection of diaphanous scarves hung from various parts of her anatomy. Her gown had a cavernous plunge neckline from which her bosom was trying hard to escape. She was busily removing the plastic cap from a bottle of vodka, a copious measure of which she poured into a paper cup, adding a raw egg and a minute measure of orange juice to the container, before tossing the mixture down her throat. Then she gave a series of vocal trills on a top C, a couple of arpeggios and a run down the scale before addressing herself to Mrs Nelligan.

'Zat is better – now I zing like the zweet birds in ze bushes,' she said in tones that could only be described as double forte. 'You will 'ave zom vodka?' she invited, looking around for another paper carton.

Mrs Nelligan shook her head, and the lady poured herself another mountainous measure which she barely diluted with some more of the fresh orange juice from a small pitcher on the dressing table.

'Gut for ze nerves and ze voice,' she said, smacking her lips and rather reluctantly capping the bottle, now reduced in level to half-way.

'I am Brunhilde Katzenhofen,' she introduced herself. 'I am Diva with leading opera company in Bavaria. I come to America to visit my brozzer who is medical doctor in New York and I agree to zing on ze television programme *Heiman's How do you do* – I zink zey call eet. Ze city air is not 'ow you zay, health making for ze impostare, zo I gargle ze glottis wiz vodka to keep ze chords lubricated!' She smiled ingenuously at Mrs Nelligan, seated herself at the dressing table, and then poured out yet another slug.

'The show', said Mrs Nelligan politely, 'is actually called *Hogan's Hello* and I am delighted to meet you. My name is Agnes Nelligan and I too am appearing on the programme.'

Brunhilde was now struggling to reach the zip fastener at the back of her dress, which Mrs Nelligan could now see was fastened to only halfway up her back.

'Allow me,' she said, and zipped the dress up to the neck,

carefully hooking the top into position. Brunhilde thanked her profusely, and then, opening her dressing case, she drew out a long rope of pearls which she wound around her neck until it made a deep collar above her dress. Even Agnes found herself impressed – the pearls were real. And as if that were not enough, Brunhilde dug into the case once more and fished out a massive looking bracelet and an ornate pearl tiara to complete the set. Obviously Bavaria paid its Divas somewhat above the salary basics.

'You tink ze zet goes wiz my dress?' Brunhilde asked anxiously. 'I 'ave ze little zet in diamond too, but I prefer to wear zem wiz my white gowns. Or I could change for ze emerald zet – how you tink?'

Agnes looked at her in amazement. 'You don't actually carry all that valuable jewellery about with you in that dressing case?' she asked.

Brunhilde shrugged. 'Why not? If I put it in ze bank, zen I cannot have it when I wish to wear it, zo I carry it wiz me.' Then she grinned. 'You tink I maybe get robbed? But would ze burglars ever tink anyone would be zo zilly as to carry zese precious stones like zo? They tink zey are only of the paste.'

Mrs Nelligan was not convinced but she realised Brunhilde was happy with her arrangements and so she had no wish to make the singer feel insecure. And as it turned out, two weeks later, she read that the singer's hotel room had been burgled and the only items not stolen but merely thrown on the ground with her stage costumes, were the pearl, diamond and emerald sets in question, so maybe Brunhilde had a point.

By now Brunhilde was trying to buckle her shoes and having some slight problem staying steady enough on her chair to do so. Agnes began to worry about her condition.

'Better let me fasten those buckles, my dear,' she said. 'Put your foot up to me. I always remember when as a small girl I had buckled shoes, I never could manage to fasten them myself. My sister always had to help me.' She smiled with infinite tact, and quickly closed the buckles. Brunhilde leaned forward and gave her an impulsive hug, tried out another scale or two and disappeared in the direction of the dressing room lavatory, from which she emerged ten minutes later, absolutely steady and bright eyed.

'I ways run ze cold water over ze wrists and arms,' she explained. 'It zends ze blood running, running, to ze head, to brighten ze brain power.' Mrs Nelligan devoutly hoped that the effects would last Brunhilde until after she had done her operatic extract, but as she was already knocking back a final helping from the vodka bottle before sailing down the corridor with one of the programme hostesses towards the studio, Agnes very much doubted the efficacy of the water treatment. Which was where she was quite wrong. Brunhilde sang like an angel, and it was only when she sat down on one of the banquette seats on the set that she quietly collapsed into a sound sleep amid the cushions, which didn't really worry anyone, since they were careful to keep her out of camera range for the first half of the show, after which she came to, and positively scintillated with an effervescent brilliance for the remainder of the telecast.

Agnes sat quietly in the dressing room, watching the opening section of the show on the television monitor. She developed a rapid respect for Daniel Hogan, who not only acted as an excellent catalyst for his guests without advancing his own views or prejudices, but also managed to control his audience with firmness and charm, so that discussions between guest and audience never got out of hand. He executed an infinitely polite hatchet job on a pretentious British peer who kept referring to his many visits to 'Glamis' in the fond illusion that his listeners were familiar with whose name it was that adorned the lease of the stately pile. Having successfully backed the plum-toned effete into a corner, Daniel then managed to discover that despite vague intimations to the contrary, the milord in question had never cracked the social circle that brought entry into Buckingham Palace parties, which rather covered the peer with some confusion. All this met with Mrs Nelligan's approval, since she never would tolerate snobbery in the young, and snobbery in the middle-aged she regarded as extreme vulgarity, only excelled by the delusions of expertise found among the pseuds in the world of wine.

At last they came to collect her and give her make-up a last flick of powder. She patted her hair with a calmness she did not really feel, and trotted down the row of shallow steps to where Daniel stood with his swivel chair, his coffee table, the mock fireplace and mantelpiece and the hooked floor-rug which the stage designer fondly imagined gave a feeling of domestic surroundings to the set.

To her infinite relief, she did not fall down the steps or trip over her feet, but it was slightly embarrassing to discover that the chair they had positioned for her to sit in was too high off the ground to be comfortable. But Daniel, like the trouper he was, turned the exchange of the chair for a lower model to advantage, when he described her as 'a little lady who will chair the biggest and most exciting project we've ever come across on this or any other programme', and with an encouraging nod, he headed Mrs Nelligan down the road to television immortality.

Chapter Eight

Mrs Nelligan was slightly bemused for the first few moments – she hadn't realised the set was going to be so bright – and her blue eyes blinked nervously at Daniel, while her mind took in her surroundings.

A young man with headphones was moving silently out of camera focus, and managing in some miraculous way, it seemed to her, to avoid tripping over the cables and slowly moving camera dollies that seemed to be approaching like Daleks from a number of corners all at once. Daniel looked slightly strange with his make-up on, but his smile was as warm and genuine as it had been during his visit to Katie's apartment and his first question eased her into a more relaxed attitude on the spot. Having introduced her to his audience, given a rundown on her teaching career and established just whereabouts in the country Hackstown was actually located, Daniel asked her to explain the proposed project of a leisure complex that owed its basics to Mr Walt Disney and its concepts to Irish mythology.

'It sounds just fascinating, the way you tell it,' said Daniel, 'and of course, of particular interest to the American people, so many of whom have their roots firmly planted in your little green isle.'

He smiled out at his several million viewers, and then Mrs Nelligan thought it was time to drop her bombshell.

'You know, Mr Hogan,' she began, fluttering her lashes in her usual timid fashion, whereupon the entire TV crew got a warm, protective feeling around its commercial heart, and a fair proportion of Daniel's viewers wanted to lean into their television screens and offer the little lady a strong arm to take hold of.

'You know, Hackstown has a very special significance for

the American people quite apart from being a part of their ancestral past.'

'Really?' said Daniel in some puzzlement, since Agnes was now veering from the general outlines of the interview.

'Yes indeed,' said Mrs Nelligan, giving him and then the cameras her widest blue-eyed look. 'The land on which we propose to establish the Tir na n-Og complex, actually belongs through a lengthy inheritance line to the wife of your very esteemed President. Mrs Randolph's family actually owned the land, going back over several hundred years. Indeed, she now holds the ancient title, a fact of which she was unaware until I visited her earlier this week to tell her that such indeed was the case. I may say she was more than pleased at the news. She was, you see, quite unaware of her close ties with Ireland and with Hackstown, and of course we are delighted that so august a personage has this important link with our village.'

She sat back in her chair and smiled gently at a flabbergasted Daniel who made great efforts to recover himself.

'Ladies and gentlemen,' he said breathlessly, 'this is total news to me I assure you. I had no idea we were going to be told this important information today ... Ma'am,' he said, turning to Mrs Nelligan in understandable excitement, 'You are *sure* about all this?'

'Certainly,' replied Mrs Nelligan. 'One of my old boys is one of Ireland's leading experts in genealogy. I have no reason to doubt his information.'

'So that means that Mrs Randolph will actually be the owner of the complex you are about to erect in Hackstown. Are you forming a partnership with her?' Daniel was genuinely puzzled.

Mrs Nelligan shook her head. 'Goodness me, no, Mr Hogan! What would the President's wife be doing mixed up in a commercial venture in Ireland? We must assume she will be much too busy for the forseeable future to concern herself with outside projects!' She laughed softly. 'No, what Mrs Randolph has most graciously and generously done, is to tell me that she will forgo her right to the land at Hackstown and donate it to the village as a gift in perpetuity, so that we may erect the complex and thus establish a permanent source of income for the locality. A most magnificent gesture, you will agree.'

Up in the control room, the director and producer were almost dancing with excitement, making wide gestures to Daniel to continue with the interview, even though out of the corner of her eye, Agnes got a glimpse of something glittering and rightly assumed that Dwane was standing by to do his Liberace impressions.

'And there will be no financial remuneration. Mrs Randolph has even promised to underwrite the legal costs of making the land over officially to Hackstown. More than that, she has also promised us a sculpture work, to be effected by her son Mr Alvin Randolph, to place in the complex as a memorial, and I know the committee will be honoured by the offer.'

Mrs Nelligan crossed her fingers for a moment and begged the forgiveness of a kindly deity for her arrant falsehood. Even the committee she proposed to get together from among Hackstown's leading citizens, would, she felt, have sufficient artistic sensitivity between them to see the horrifics of Alvin's endeavours.

'You know, ma'am,' said Daniel happily, 'our telephone lines are all jammed up with calls to the show. Your news has quite taken our viewers by surprise. They want to know the full story of how you discovered that our President's wife has genuine Irish roots, and they want to hear all about the complex and what it is going to look like. As a matter of fact we already have enquiries about vacation bookings!'

Mrs Nelligan chuckled. 'I think all that would take rather longer than we have time available,' she said, and Daniel got back on their interview track once more.

'Well ma'am, there's no way we're going to let you leave things as they are, so you'd surely please all of us if you could come back again tomorrow and talk with us some more.'

'I would be only too delighted,' replied Agnes and settled herself comfortably in her chair, as Daniel introduced, with considerable reluctance, an impatient Dwane, who bounced on to the set with a smile as wide as a melon slice and promptly threw his arms around the now awakened Brunhilde, planting a smacking kiss on her surprised cheek and then racing smartly to the vocal troupe which was composed of three statuesque coloured vocalists decked out in electric-blue satin catsuits, topped by matching blue feather boas. Unfortunately, Dwane got a mouthful of boa as he grasped the middle singer around her waist, which was as high as he could reach, seeing that she was six feet tall and already standing on a dais. A feather which went down his throat rather spoiled the effect of his kissing session as he coughed his way towards Mrs Nelligan, and then recalling her previous activities in the canteen, Dwane wisely drew back and sat down beside Daniel.

While Daniel explained that Dwane was a favoured finalist for the 'Junior America Talent and Charm' contest, Mrs Nelligan solicitously banged him on the back, handed him a glass of water, and obligingly fixed his bow-tie which again had swivelled to starboard. After all, she quite liked his mother.

Dwane made a commendable recovery and then, turning to Mrs Nelligan, he placed what he believed was a confiding chubby hand on her shoulder.

She promptly removed it.

'Gee ma'am, I've been listening to what you said about your home town and it sure sounds keen – has Hickstown got cute little old piggies and baby rabbits and have you ever seen a real live leprechaun?' Dwane looked earnestly into camera One, pushing out his lower lip just like he had watched Freddie Bartholemew do in the old home-movies his mother had hired for him to learn from about childish charm and appeal.

Mrs Nelligan closed her eyes and when she reopened them, Daniel was surprised at the steel-blue look he saw in their depths.

'*Ha*ckstown,' she said clearly, emphasising the first two letters of the village's name – and it was an action she would repeat many times before she finally got the pronunciation through to the great American public – 'Hackstown has its acceptable complement of animals, and no, I have not seen a leprechaun – up to the present time!' And she smiled into

Dwane's face, set in its well-practised questioning look. Daniel sniggered involuntarily as Dwane suddenly blanched and turned a slightly hunted gaze to the side of the set where his mother was standing. Daniel hastily suggested that Dwane might like to do one of his impressions and as he launched into a take-off of Donny Osmond, which he managed to render exactly half a tone off key from the piano accompaniment provided by a piano player with an agonised expression, Dwane was mercifully overrun by the screen credits and by Daniel reminding his viewers to 'relax and stay cool' for the rest of the day.

Mrs Nelligan was surrounded by an excited studio team when the show came off the air. Daniel's production assistant was even now pursuing her with a new appearance contract, and Daniel, putting an arm around her, guided her into a corner of the show's hospitality room, poured her a pale sherry, and wagged an admonishing finger at her.

'Naughty, naughty lady,' he said with a grin. 'Upstaging poor Daniel like that! But it made a heck of a show – and I suppose you were quite aware that it would?'

Mrs Nelligan looked apologetically at him. 'I do hope you are not cross with me, Mr Hogan,' she fluttered. 'But I felt it would be much more interesting for you if I told you – well – spontaneously, as it were. The element of total surprise, you know.' She blinked her eyelashes at him and he gave her an unexpected kiss on her pink cheek.

'I think it was great – we'll get more mileage out of it tomorrow and we'll start the Pledge bit on tomorrow's show. I can see this taking off at a real fast rate – the public loves a television marathon. Our Investathon will be a winner, just you wait and see. After today, who could resist investing in Hickstown?' Mrs Nelligan sighed. 'Sorry, Hackstown,' said Daniel.

'Oh I do so hope you are right, Mr Hogan,' fluted Mrs Nelligan as she caught sight of Katie pressing her way through the crowd, ready to take her aunt in tow. Jonathan suddenly appeared in the doorway and cut a sudden swathe through the bodies to catch Katie by the arm in what her aunt could only see as a most proprietory fashion.

'Come to dinner and we'll celebrate your success on the

show,' he invited, and Katie raised enquiring brows at Mrs Nelligan. 'Thank you, my dear Jonathan, but perhaps a glass of sherry, and then you can call me a taxi. I am sorry, I mean a cab. I feel a little weary. But I know Katie will be free, we have no firm commitments for the evening,' she said giving her niece a gentle warning pressure of her elbow.

Katie demurred but her aunt would have none of it. 'My dear Katie, you have a full refrigerator. I am perfectly capable of cutting up some cold chicken and preparing a salad for myself. After all, I do live alone in Hackstown! It will be nice to see the programme again on your clever recording machine. Really, progress is wonderful. I intend to invest in a video machine when I return home; it would be delightful to view all the old films I enjoyed years ago. The type being shown today are a positive embarrassment!'

'Ah,' said Daniel, overhearing her last remarks, 'a romantic at heart, Mrs Nelligan! Do you long for *Camille* or *The Sheik*?'

'Not at all,' replied Agnes with some asperity. 'It would be nice to see *Rio Bravo* or *The Magnificent Seven* or even *The Lavender Hill Mob* again. I simply cannot have patience with the current trend of using the naked body to sidetrack one's awareness of the massive inadequacies of the majority of modern plots. Not only is it boring in the extreme, but denigrating to the intelligent cinema-goer. I have always believed that the human body is at its most appealing when clothed, and at its most ridiculous when naked!'

'My,' commented Daniel in some admiration. 'That is an area we should explore a little further when we have you back on the show. Or even on another occasion when we could have some of the film critics along to do battle. Would you be prepared to take them on?'

Mrs Nelligan smiled. 'Why not? I might give them something to think about – I held classes in film and drama appreciation when I taught school. I don't expect their arguments would be unfamiliar to me.'

They found a comfortable hostelry near the studios and Daniel ordered her the pale dry sherry she favoured, and a Canadian Club whiskey for himself. As they sipped their drinks, he expanded his ideas for the Investathon.

'We've lined up six well-known stage and movie stars to man the telephone bank in the studios, to take the pledges for Hackstown,' he said. 'They will do a two-hour stretch and will then be relieved by six more new personalities. The names will be flashed up on the TV screen so that viewers can talk to their own favourite instead of being plugged in to any of the personalities at random. It might be a good exercise for calculating the personal popularity stakes of any star, as their agents will quickly realise! Do you know, we have offers of stars from three agencies already, all of them top names willing to take part and prepared to donate their fee to a named charity. That means we don't raise any hackles and we keep the do-gooders happy. We'll keep the phone lines open for two days after which we shut shop and at the end of the week we have our draw for the winner of the free trip to stay at the complex when it goes up.'

'Splendid,' said Mrs Nelligan. 'And of course, the trip will be a luxury one – fly over on the Concorde, the use of a Rolls Royce while in Ireland, and we will make quite sure the winner of the holiday will find the Sword of Finn McCool when he or she goes on an archeological dig!'

'Why Aunt Agnes, I thought you were a purist and now I find you tolerating phony artefacts and the trappings of capitalism!' grinned Katie as she gathered her handbag and gloves before departing with Jonathan for the promised dinner which turned out to be completely forgettable as to what they consumed, but memorable for the fact that she fell in love with her host, quite totally and completely, by the time they reached the coffee stage.

'Oh but I am ... in most areas ...' retorted her aunt calmly. 'The really important things in life should be treated with respect, and a proper regard for the fitness of things is what makes them endure and survive the philistines of this world. But when they can be utilised for the greater good, then they have a genuine purpose in the scheme of things.' She looked earnestly at her niece and then winked.

'That's a first-class girl, your niece,' commented Daniel as he watched his son escort Katie through the swing doors of the cocktail bar, with a mesmerised care which Jonathan hadn't brought to a female of any sort since he was nine and his pet rabbit, a chincilla doe named Beckie, delivered herself of her first litter of young.

'Yes, isn't she?' replied Agnes.

'It's about time my lad was settling down and getting serious about life and where he's going,' said Daniel ruminatively. 'What he needs is a good steadying hand, preferably female and attached to a sensible girl – like Katie, for instance.'

'Exactly what I believe too, in reverse, of course,' said Mrs Nelligan. 'I'm sure Jonathan is a fine and upstanding young man and Katie is all you say, but career or no career, every young woman needs a strong and steady husband to lean on, don't you think?'

And they smiled at each other in perfect agreement.

Chapter Nine

The newspapers were a publicist's dream next day and thanks to the inevitable leak from the studios, Katie's boutique was besieged by journalists looking for a follow-up story. But by agreement, Agnes had declared she was giving no interviews; the entire coverage was to be effected on Daniel's show, at least until the full brunt of the Investathon got off the ground. After that, hopefully, it was open season for coverage.

In the two days prior to her return visit to *Hogan's Hello* and the start of the Investathon, Agnes was almost permanently engaged on the telephone, during which time a considerable number of her 'old boys' contacted her with eager offers of financial assistance to launch Hackstown into the tourist world in style. She had a quick plane flight to Texas where she viewed Alan's aforesaid oil wells and accepted the projected profits for a twelvemonth of one of the smaller wells which would keep Hackstown's complex in little items like light, heating and transportation for the next couple of years. The accountants would, Alan assured her, bank the returns on a simple transfer system which would guarantee the minimum amount in advance with a settlement at the end of the year of all outstanding profits. It would be a sort of collateral, when she went dollar-bargaining elsewhere, he pointed out.

Since she was already in Texas, Agnes flipped across to visit her old boy with the vast acreage under cattle – a subject on which she was better versed, coming from a farming community like Hackstown, than she was about oil.

Dear David, she told Katie when she telephoned her niece, had asked her to pick out a top-grade steer, ostensibly to test her knowledge of beef on the hoof, and when she had unerringly settled on the pride of his very considerable herd, he had isolated it, added another hundred like it, and held a cattle auction to swell the Hackstown fund by several hundred thousand dollars more. He had also held a perfectly delightful barbecue to introduce her to his friends. The Texans, Mrs Nelligan confided, did things in a big way and had extremely big hearts, matched, she had to confess, by the size of their concept of themselves. But it was, she said, perhaps a little cavalier to complain since the same big-hearted friends of dear David formed an investment group among themselves and were working out a little something or other for Hackstown. They said it was just a little exercise in relaxation from their more high-powered corporate operations!

By the time she returned to New York, Daniel had the big show well lined up. It had gained considerable extra time not to mention content, since he had first conceived it. By now they had twenty high-school majorettes and twelve professional harpists, in kelly green cloaks and red skirts with white broderie-anglaise aprons and silver-buckled shoes, lined up to do a four-minute musical spot. They had three leading movie stars with solid Irish backgrounds of only the first generation, booked for an in-depth interview on the Romanticism of Ireland, and a leading travel writer was still recovering from the jet lag sustained by a fast twenty-four-hour whistle-stop tour of all the best-known Irish beauty spots. The top Irish dancing club in the Bronx had contributed four of its best dancers who were all set to do a hornpipe, a slipjig and a four-hand reel, aided by an immigrant from Galway who was an inspired performer on the tin whistle. The studio had a bank of telephones each with its own dais which was topped by a perspex canopy decorated with flashing coloured lights which were to light up each time a call with a pledge came through the main switchboard.

The set designer had had a wonderful time. He had designed a backdrop in satin, which he constructed into a collage of thatched cottages, blue skies and green mountains. He was in ecstasies over yet another little gimmick he was organising. He had hired two little donkeys which he was about to dress in a bright green harness with two Irish turf creel baskets into which, at intervals, the pretty hostesses keeping score on the phoned-in pledges would drop dockets which carried on them the promised amounts and details of the donors.

He wanted an excuse to bring the animals on to the set regularly, during the entire show. He had seen the turf-hauling donkeys years back on the only trip he had ever made through Ireland, which was actually a stop over at Shannon when he was en route to Europe to the Monte Carlo film festival, and he had never forgotten their charm. The fact that the animals had the uncharming habit of crapping at regular intervals, and would very likely do so on the studio floor, completely escaped him, and it took treble time and 'embarrassment money' to the union of studio maintenance workers concerned to pacify its members later, when they had to follow the animals with pans and pooper-scoopers.

They tried in the wardrobe department to inveigle Mrs Nelligan into an Irish traditional Kinsale cloak until with infinite patience, considerable forbearance and commendable restraint, she told them that she simply hadn't the height for it, informing them quite mendaciously that Kinsale women were all six feet tall and built accordingly. Katie produced a delightful lemon yellow chiffon that made Agnes look as appealing and vulnerable as an Easter chick straight out of the egg, and it fitted in nicely with the preponderance of greens with which the set was being adorned.

Agnes viewed the preparations with horrified incredulity; the supreme ability of these well-meaning, good natured, ethnically blinkered people to mount an extravaganza of such supreme schmaltz and tastelessness, passed her understanding. Jonathan apologetically tried to explain it all to her. They had, he told her, to give the public what the sponsors decided it wanted to be given. It would be the same if she happened to came from Hawaii, an Indian reservation, or the Highlands of Scotland. She would have ended up swamped by Hula skirts, tomahawks and feathers

85

or haggis and nylon sporrans, and she therefore had to be grateful, he said sadly, that the producer didn't put in a demand for a team of midgets which he could dress up as Irish leprechauns.

'Never mind,' he consoled. 'Just think of all those lovely money pledges that will come in and you'll feel a lot better!'

However, Daniel did have one nice surprise for her. His bonus item was a short colour video of Hackstown, its environs, and the locality of the proposed Tir na n-Og which he had had filmed when the travel writer was making his breakneck tour around the other beauty spots. She felt quite nostalgic when she watched it come up on the monitor. The Castle Court Hotel window boxes, she thought, came across particularly well, and the white painted sign of the Hackstown Gun Club looked as if the Major had recently had it repainted – probably in defiance of her proposals. In fact, she noticed that the Club committee had been doing a deal of work in her absence: there was a new barbed-wire fence round the club house area. The video cameraman had certainly filmed the area with a keen eye for its scenic beauty. It had a rather 'other world' look to it, particularly the evening shots of the lake where the marsh gases were billowing slightly in a quite ethereal way. One almost expected to see a troupe of Little People scampering down the narrow pathway which, in actual fact, was a cattle track to the lake shore for drinking purposes. Even the studio personnel were heard to sigh with a slightly yearning sound as the video was being shown, pleasing Daniel who realised that if he touched the hardened professionals, God alone knew what extreme favourable effect it would all have on his public.

Mrs Nelligan told the viewers of the ambitions of Hackstown to do its own thing in the world of big business and then launched into the tale of how she had discovered the First Lady's connections.

Within seconds it was quite surprising how many viewers suddenly discovered similar links with the village. They jammed the telephones, all of them longing to discuss their roots with Mrs Nelligan and just aching, it appeared, to invest in the survival plans of their ancestral locale. And for those who could not properly or even improperly claim kinship with Hackstown, but had to rely on perimeters up to a hundred miles away from the locality, the inspired catch phrase, coined by a truck driver who called in from Nebraska asking to be allowed to 'Buy a Bit of Ireland' became the operative slogan for the entire project.

On the dais, the lights were flashing at a fast rate, the hostesses were hurriedly scribbling tallies for the donkey creels, and at regular intervals, with the drum majorettes parading across the set in their natty white boots, the placards gave the running total of the pledges. The Hogan Investathon was well under way, and it gained further impetus when Mrs Nelligan's old boy Ambrose 'Bobo' Carter, of the west-coast television organisation, telephoned in personally to talk to his ex-schoolteacher, and promised her a back-up service from his own company. Indeed, Bobo was so enthusiastically eager to help that even Daniel was impressed.

Perhaps the most important backing group the Hackstown project gained was the support of the major American gun clubs, who in a rapid series of decisions decided, due to a slight confusion on their part, that it was their bounden duty to help a fellow club in its hour of financial extremity. Immediately pleading their considerably powerful support officially, on television, through the offices of their New York chapter President, they were, they told Agnes, fully prepared to give every assistance, both financial and practical, professional and political, to get the complex going.

Mrs Nelligan, accepting with her usual grace, refused to think what the Association would say or do when its officers discovered that they were aiding and assisting in the demise of an affiliated sporting concern, whose charter encouraged its faithful to take pot shots at anything feathered that was ill-advised enough to wing its way around the area, but she put the thought firmly out of her mind.

It was to be expected that some souls of the entertainment world would turn the Hackstown Investathon to their own advantage. Which accounted for the fading musical comedy star who turned up in a white limousine complete with a floor-length mink coat which she donated to be auctioned on the show, with the proceeds to go to the Tir na n-Og fund. A well-known pop-music idol had the same idea in mind when he arrived with the offer of one of his smaller holiday homes situated on the island of Mustique. There was, it could be appreciated, every chance of sharing a section of beach with some of the world's leading VIPs for the lucky winner. And the idea of a television auction seemed to grow like Topsy, when yet another famous face turned up, this time from the popular romantic novel world, with the offer of a diamond cabochon ring, whose carats were enough to make a good dent in the Irish National Debt.

Daniel delightedly announced that the sale would take place at the end of the following week with outside bids accepted only by telephone direct to the show. And he would, he told his viewers, be pleased to accept a few bits and pieces to add to the loot already in hand. Within two hours, they had to close the list of offerings from a public whose main aim in life appeared to be the salvation of Hackstown. Daniel had valuable paintings, silverware, a quite superior emerald pendant, a block of gilt-edged shares in a new condominium about to go up on Long Island, a rather splendid little motor cruiser moored in its own boathouse down in Acapulco, with an attached cosy little beach cabin. He had the offer of a custom-built white sports car whose cocktail cabinet had real gold-plated dispenser units and cut-glass bottles; while among the minor contributions were offers of swimming pool installations, total home refurnishing vouchers, tickets for a cruise to Europe, a whole weekend at South Fork ranch and a rare opportunity to see Sue Ellen's lip tremble at close quarters.

Agnes and her Irish Wonderland had quite taken over the American public imagination, and the spin-off by way of political leverage come election time had not escaped the personnel of the White House. 'Jimmy' James Stafford was consequently even more respectful than usual when he contacted Mrs Nelligan to arrange for the little ceremony in Washington, at which the First Lady would hand over the deed of gift in an appropriate speech which, Jimmy said, would lean on the importance of her own Irish roots, bestowed, as it were, almost first-hand on her husband through a happy matrimonial affiliation which was, she intended to suggest, solid enough to overlook the fact that he hadn't a drop of Gaelic blood in the smallest vein of his body.

She would not be dwelling on those non-Irish origins of her husband, Jimmy hastened to add, if she could find a non-contentious point of common reference about his British roots, which in no way could be used against him by the Opposition. Mrs Nelligan suggested that the First Lady keep off the actual Irish forebears issue and emphasise the fact that being an American President made the holder of the office a sort of Uni-National figure – what one might call the living version of the Unknown or Universal Soldier – in which case no one would be uncivil enough to use the President's roots as a means of fouling up his prospects among the Irish American voters, either on or off the political fence. The fact that this was precisely what the First Lady did indicates how deep an impression Mrs Nelligan had made on her when they met. And events being as they were, the introduction of Mrs Nelligan to the First Lady stood 'Jimmy' James Stafford in very good stead, because the following year the President elevated Jimmy to greater heights of Public Relations power, when the Randolphs got a new lease on the White House for a further four-year term.

Mrs Nelligan's flight to Washington for the second time since her arrival in America was rather different from the first. She was accompanied by a sizeable Press Corps and a TV crew from Daniel's sponsors, who by now were feeling more than a little proprietory about the entire operation of establishing a fairyland in Hackstown. (In fact rumour was already strong that the President of the Company intended to book a permanent apartment in the new complex when it went up. At that stage no one had broken it to him that the beehive huts which Agnes envisaged were going to be quite basic, when it came to mod. cons. It was only when his wife heard there wasn't going to be a jacuzzi in every room that he had to forget the whole idea.)

'Jimmy' James was there to meet them, escort them to

their destinations and provide their press passes, information sheets, publicity kits and invitations to lunch before the return trip to New York. The First Lady looked delightful in a pale green suit of silk tweed, which, if the truth were known, never had its creation on an Irish loom, but which nevertheless kept the mood of the occasion. On the steps of the White House, she made her graceful speech of welcome, presentation and donation, and amid a battery of press and television cameras, Mrs Nelligan received the deeds of Hackstown Gun Club preserve with more than a small modicum of triumph in her heart. A slightly confused President emerged for a moment to shake her hand, thank her for whatever she was supposed to have done, and hope she would enjoy the hospitality of the United States, before disappearing thankfully indoors again. Mrs Nelligan released another gem for publication as she closed her handbag on the important document with its green silk ribbon ties. ('Jimmy' James had a great eye for relativities.)

'It is said,' she told the press corps confidingly, 'that Christopher Columbus came to Ireland before he discovered your great country. There is a local tale in Hackstown which has been passed down from generation to generation around the cottage fires, that Columbus sent an emissary from his ship to the village of Hackstown to employ a young carpenter as his shipwright when he was about to sail on to what became the New World. The young carpenter was renowned for his workmanship and his young wife was considered to be the most beautiful girl in the county with Titian-red hair long enough for her to sit on. They are said to have sailed with Columbus to America and the story has it that it is one of their descendants who ultimately returned to Ireand and occupied the Abbeyfield lands, to which your President's gracious wife has now relinquished her title. It is, of course, only an old legend, but we in Hackstown like to think that, like all stories, it has a firm foundation in fact.' And she glanced at the beaming First Lady whose dark red tresses seemed to take on a sudden new glow, as the point of Mrs Nelligan's little story began to sink home.

It was the perfect end to a publicity-loaded occasion, and

there was hardly a television set across the country which was not tuned into Daniel Hogan's programme next evening to view what had now become an ongoing saga as compulsive as *Dallas*.

Mrs Nelligan felt like a movie star as she stepped out of the studio car before the Big Show (as Jonathan had begun to term the programme) was due for transmission. There was a massive queue of ticket holders waiting to get in, and an equally massive queue in a railed-off area outside the building, waiting to see who was going in. Her arrival gained a faltering burst of cheering and an elegant blond-haired young man leaned across the barrier as she was passing and pushed a long envelope into her hand, carefully turning his left profile around so that his best side was photographed by the cameraman who materialised by his side in a miraculous fashion.

'Read it, lady, and I'll be in touch. We're makin' you an offer you won't refuse, I sure hope,' he said rapidly. Later, when she perused the contents of the letter, she found he represented 'Heimie's Irish Pizza Cabins', a chain of fast-food takeaways in the Bronx, and they were offering Mrs Nelligan considerable amounts of money to endorse the product of the unlikely alliance between a Jewish bakery, an Italian recipe and a culture which had only recently discovered the world of instant cookery. Her refusal to participate when the young man telephoned her later was seen for evermore by himself and his directors as a prime example of the vagaries of the crazy Irish who didn't recognise a good deal when it was offered.

Heimie's Irish Pizza Cabins did, however, manage to cream off some undeserved publicity when the photo taken by the young man's photographer eventually found its way into one of the morning papers, and the enterprising Heimie announced to those interested that the photo had been taken on the occasion the firm had made a donation, on behalf of all its customers with Irish affiliations, to the Hackstown fund. Hopefully, he announced, in the years to come, the Irish franchise for Heimie's Pizzas would be negotiated, so that American visitors to Hackstown's Tir na n-Og would still be able to avail themselves of the joys which

Heimie's firm cooked up for them at the bakeries in the Bronx.

Mrs Nelligan was fascinated by the Investathon procedures, as she sat with Daniel throughout the show. The telephones ran constantly, the dais lights blinked in a rainbow of colours, the efficient young ladies kept trotting about with slips of paper bearing pledges, and at regular intervals a couple in unlikely-looking Irish costumes led on the two donkeys with their creels full of promissory slips, which then went to a trio of official scrutineers at a computer bank, who fed in the figures and then watched the total display come up on the screen with an excitement that was more enthusiastically sustained than any games show compère could have done.

Off set, Mrs Nelligan could see a frantic floor manager waving at his assistants to make with the sawdust and brushes, as the donkeys, who had been (ill-advisedly) well fed and watered before the show, in the hope that the meal would keep them quiet, now eliminated what they no longer needed – unfortunately, smack in the centre of the passageway from the dressing rooms to the set, and he was again having difficulty in persuading the crew to remove the obstruction before someone walked in it. By the time he reached an agreement, someone had.

But it was a small cloud on an otherwise brilliantly blue horizon, and by the end of the Investathon, Daniel's computer crew were exultantly announcing they were well over the million-dollar mark and the night was still very young, as Mr Hogan reminded his viewers. And of course, the auction was still to come.

Agnes was going to be there, much as she would, by now, have prefered to be elsewhere. She was getting no sightseeing done and very little shopping to bring back to Hackstown with her. But, Daniel pointed out, she was a main link and, as such, there was no way the proceedings would have the same impact if she were to vacate the comfortable velvet-covered armchair which, after two shows, was almost the Nelligan trademark on camera.

What Daniel's sponsors were now billing as the 'Rainbow's End Auction' was scheduled for the second-last show the following week, so that Daniel could do a little extra promoting and entice more of the well-heeled into the studio for the actual auction. This, he reasoned, would give good competition to those bidding by telephone and it would also be a gala 'invitation only' occasion. He wasn't proposing to act as official auctioneer himself, but he opted instead to describe the items up for sale and a host of beautiful showgirls each dressed in one of the rainbow colours would bring in the item or its reference documents, as each lot came up for bidding on. It was, the set designer told everyone, going to be the most beautiful and artistic spectacular on television by the time he had completed his plans. The sponsors, dazzled by new ratings far beyond their dreams, somewhat rashly agreed to give what amounted to an open cheque to meet production costs. Hackstown-itis had gotten to them also.

Even though she would be returning to Ireland after the auction was over, Mrs Nelligan was already committed to an early return to New York. Not only had she promised to come back on *Hogan's Hello*, once she had given the good news to the village and the complex committee, but she was also expected to pay another call on the First Lady so that Mrs Randolph could keep herself up to date on her ex-inheritance. Agnes could see that the First Lady was likely to become a minor nuisance – she might have handed over her land but she didn't part with the authority that went with it quite so readily. Still, Mrs Nelligan consoled herself, once things got under way, America could be quite a fair old distance from County Meath and her village. And once it came to the American election campaign, the F.L. would have plenty to occupy her without bothering about a few acres of bogland. Mrs Nelligan reminded herself to remember to include a nightly prayer for the Presidential success of her benefactor, once she got back home.

Chapter Ten

Now, not everyone in New York was enchanted with the campaign to save Hackstown village. In fact there were a fair few who surveyed all the publicity, the fuss and especially the returns from the Investathon, with teeth gritted hard enough to crack the toughest walnut. Sadly, the milk of human kindess and the urge to share possessions with the under-privileged are not common to all the human race. The détente between the Irish and the Italians, on the grounds that Roman Catholic nations should stick together, stopped short among the New York Number Four section of the East Side Mafia. To their local Capo, Mr Pius 'Torch' Donelli, – so called because of his youthful preference for using a powerful police flashlight with which to blind his victims before he shot them carefully in the guts, in the days when he was a hit man for one of the Chicago Families – the National Leader, sent word that they were less than happy with events of the moment.

Nowadays, of course, Pius was respectable and hired accountants and lawyers to eliminate the competition. He was head of a society called the Associates of American Democracy, which was a combination of the Cosa Nostra, the Ku Klux Klan, and the Friendly Sons of St Brigid – unlikely bedfellows who operated most amicably together, each of them staying firmly out of the other's commercial patch, only coming together when it became possible that their combined plans might be in danger of being jeopardised by some outside influence which none of them could handle. It seemed to all three of them that the loss of large amounts of good solid American dollars to a hamlet of Irish shmucks was a consummation devoutly to be avoided at any cost.

The officers of the Friendly Sons, therefore, having seen that they need expect no help from the Republican gun clubs who had publicly pledged their support to the Hackstown project, were more than relieved when their Chief Executive was contacted by Mr Donelli at a surprisingly early hour for 'Torch' to be about, on the day after the Investathon of *Hogan's Hello*.

Mr Jamesey Quilligan was also President of the Gaelic Trust and Investment Corporation. His organisation insured most of the Catholic church property, the domiciles of the Irish in the Bronx and Irish-owned businesses on the west side of town, as well as a sizeable chunk of the Italian-owned commercial properties which his associates put in his way. He was still only at the oatmeal stage of his morning repast when Torch telephoned.

'Quilligan!' Torch bellowed down the telephone. Naturally basso profundo voiced, he had never come to terms with the workings of the communications world and still in his heart believed that people only heard you down the wire if you shouted into the receiver as loudly as possible. It made for constant neuralgia pains for his secretary, and were it not for the pair of jewelled earmuffs which his current mistress designed and insisted on his having made up for her at Tiffany's, Torch would have found it difficult to occupy his limited leisure hours, since it was no longer practical for him to visit public places such as theatres, libraries, art galleries and museums. By which it can be gathered that Torch spent long periods on the business telephone.

Jamesey put the telephone on the table with a shudder of panic as Torch's voice assailed his consciousness before he had drowned the Bloody Mary and coffee which daily followed the porridge his wife insisted he consume to 'set him up for the day', as she regularly told him. He stood well back, fumbling for his glass, and having swallowed the contents he sat down and poured out his coffee, while Torch's voice emerged quite clearly down the phone from half-way across the dining room.

'Quilligan – thisa Hickstown woman and her funda raising game – the Familia, they don'ta like it, they don'ta like it at all, capisc'?'

Quilligan capisced very well. Someone was already leaning on Torch who in turn was about to lean on Jamesey.

'What did Buzz Baumann think?' he asked, moving carefully to the telephone, and having asked his question, shoved the receiver well away from his ear again.

'You know whatta he say ever' time – if it don'ta have niggers ina da story, Buzz couldn'ta care less. But he tolda me he woulda be on oura side, ifa we maka da move to do somethin' about thisa crazy Irisha woman.' When he got worked up, Torch reverted to thinking in his native tongue which made his instant translation into the vernacular an exercise in concentration for his listeners.

The gentleman under discussion, one Mr Buzz Baumann, was the co-ordinator of the local branch of the Ku Klux Klan and a loving father of four daughters. A son he never talked about was very happily married to a beautiful Jewish girl and had further compounded what his father declared was arch treachery by adopting a set of coloured twin girls to whom Buzz's wife was devoted. It was not the best of moments to elicit support from Mr Baumann since he had his own little problems. His second daughter was at this moment about to marry a Polish boy whose family were staunchly Catholic, and Buzz was worried about the reactions of his fellow Klansmen, who, to be honest, nowadays only donned their robes for the annual Christmas party, and never even contemplated taking burning crosses out on the local freeways. But he felt it was quite out of line for the leader to have such skeletons in his family cupboard and it was stretching Klansmen's loyalty a bit far to expect them to tolerate these loudly rattling bones. So his annoyance level against an Irish financial rip-off of a floating dollar Shangri-La, was not as high as Torch would have liked. Still, two out of three in the group wasn't bad and he could rely on Jamesey to make equal efforts to stop the flow of good convertible American dollars from leaving the country where the power of the Mafia and the Friendly Sons could cream off the bulk of it more easily. As long as the Sons of St Brigid got their cut for personal and charitable distributions, they didn't ask for protracted audits of the books, preferring to leave the Final Accounting to Providence itself – which suited the Cosa Nostra down to the ground.

'What do you want to do about it?' asked Jamesey, now beginning to come to normality, thanks to a second Bloody Mary and four spoons of sugar in his coffee.

'We musta stop this crazy woman froma having the money away. That mucha money could be useful to the Familia's plans – dey hava tolda me to get ita sorted out,' replied Torch.

'Well, you've got an office full of accountants and lawyers to advise you. I'm no legal expert,' wheezed Jamesey, fighting for breath as he lit up his first cigarette of the day.

Torch waited until he recovered from his bout of coughing. 'I keepa tellin' you tha you oughtta smoka da cigars – cigarettes isa goin' a kill you off before you get to holda your daughter's bambini,' Mr Donelli remonstrated. He himself preferred to place an unlit Corona between his teeth and chew on it until it disintegrated. In fact Torch had never lit a stogie since he was ten years old and had burned the end of his nose with a paper spill while having a forbidden smoke under his bed. The resulting fire at his home when he dropped the spill and raced to the bathroom for the water tap, leaving the paper to set the mattress alight, had taught him the folly of inhaling the dreaded nicotine. It had also separated him permanently from his parents, because the police eventually decided that Torch was a ten-year-old arsonist, and put him into reform school until he was eighteen, by which time his father and mother had lost interest and moved back to the Italian village in Sicily where his grandparents lived.

'What they woulda do legal, woulda taka too long, – the cash woulda be outta da country well before they woulda geta da finger out – you know whatta da legal klatch is,' said Torch. 'I thinka we coulda do somethin' ourselves – you an' me. You be ina your office thisa mornin' an' I stop by around noon.'

'You have a plan?' asked Jamesey hopefully, because inventive Mr Quilligan was not.

'Sure I gotta plan,' replied Mr Donelli irritably. 'You tinka I spenda my time calling you to talka about da weather?'

And a plan he certainly had. The only problem about it was to convince the cautious Jamesey that it was viable. After all, as Mr Quilligan pointed out, he had things pretty good in Gaelic Trust and Investment Corporation, and the Friendly Sons of St Brigid were also a valuable political asset – why should he rock his own boat?

'Because ifa you don'ta help, the Familia will personally see to it that the Gaelic Trust getsa no more Italian business. And there's ever' chance that the wild ones of the Familia coulda arrange it so thata you geta some heavy fire-insurance claims on a couple of youra properties!' explained Torch reasonably.

Jamesey subsided, anxiously working out whether it would be better to be made bankrupt by the Mafia or the supporters of Noraid. He hadn't quite decided by the end of the meeting, but obediently made a few telephone calls to interested newspapers. Which was why certain publications headlined what they termed the 'Irish Terrorist inspired financial rip-off of American capital', perpetrated on a gullible American public by *Hogan's Hello*. It was suggested that, far from financing an Irish Fairyland leisure complex in Hackstown village, the cash was destined for the continental armaments vendors, whose wares, the newspapers declared, would ultimately depart to Ireland's troubled northern province, addressed to the terrorist protestors and wrapped in free balaclavas.

Naturally, the source of the information was protected by the authors, but it caused no little annoyance to the studios, the sponsors and Mrs Nelligan, who prided herself on being totally apolitical throughout her professional life.

Daniel was irate because his office wasted valuable time taking hundreds of phone calls about the Hackstown Fund. Indeed, some of the more important contributors who had leanings towards a place in the Senate or were watching for vacancies in the House of Representatives actually talked of withdrawing their pledges, and it was taking hours of sweet talk to cool the situation.

Mrs Nelligan decided she would have to find out who the perpetrator of the rumour was, and it was indeed fortunate that one of her 'boys' owned a major share in a leading newspaper publishing house. It was therefore a simple matter for her to telephone him and have him run down the source through his own channels of authority. She told Daniel what she had discovered, and being a little more knowledgeable than he about the activities at home and abroad of the Sons of St Brigid, Agnes realised why the Associates of American Democracy were getting out their knives for her plan. She did a little research on Mr Donelli.

The willing assistance of the Head of Administration and Liaison downtown at the headquarters of the New York force of law and order, who had once been a pupil at the Academy for Young Gentlemen, provided her with a good deal of background on Torch. The police, her 'old boy' told her, had tried hard for many years to return Pius to the land of his forebears, with little success. Torch wasn't keen on Sicily: the money wasn't great there, even for a Capo, and anyway, the Old Country was for retiring to, escaping from the law to, or for being married in. Torch was not yet ready for the vineyard in the sun, or dumb enough to give the police sufficient reason to come down on him, or brave enough to shake off his current wife in order to find a new and virginal young Italian girl of good Sicilian mafia background. He liked America; his financial roots were there and they were firm enough to keep him one jump ahead of the extradition orders. But the police lived in hope of finding something good enough to pin on Torch one day.

Mrs Nelligan was devoted to Italian culture and regularly enjoyed her three weeks on the Italian Riviera every June when the school holidays came around. She felt that the country, even if it was Torch's place of origin, could well do without his presence. Italy's gain might be America's loss, but America was bigger and better able to assimilate the deficit. She decided that Mr Donelli should be co-opted to the side of Hackstown.

As a visiting Irish tourist, she thought, a call on the Society to pay her respects to the Friendly Sons of the female patron saint of Ireland would not be misconstrued.

She trotted into the imposing glass structure which housed the organisation, taking the elevator to the penthouse where the Associates of American Democracy had its head-quarters, with a view over the city which was quite breathtaking – not that Torch took an artistic interest. It was merely that he felt safer on the top of the pile, believing that forty-seven stories up was too much for the malcontents to bother to bomb – a theory which was probably correct.

Torch's receptionist, an avid TV watcher, recognised Mrs Nelligan immediately and dropped her emery nail-file in genuine pleasure when Agnes approached her desk.

'Gee, Mrs Nelligan, I saw you on the Hogan show – you sure did terrific with all that money for your project,' she exclaimed, her fashion-conscious eye taking in the hand-kerchief-linen suit in palest green with its soft tan accessories which Mrs Nelligan was wearing, and mentally stashing the look away for a future trip to Bloomingdales.

'Thank you,' said Mrs Nelligan politely, observing the lady, whose name on a plaque at the front of her desk read 'Ms Maguire', noting that she was over forty, overweight and over blonde.

'I just *love* the Irish,' gushed Ms Maguire. 'My grandparents came from Ireland – from Tralee. County Galway, I believe, though I've never been to Ireland myself. I keep planning to go – maybe on my next honeymoon.' Ms Maguire smiled rather reminiscently. 'My first honeymoon I spent in Acapulco which was very classy. My second, we went to Squaw Valley to see the winter Olympics.' She frowned. 'Now that was my mistake – the no-good I was fool enough to marry fell for an ice-skater and left me flat – on my honeymoon, can you imagine?' Mrs Nelligan looked suitably shocked.

'And what's more,' Ms Maguire went on, 'I had to settle the bill in the hotel. He hadn't even got the decency to pay before he took off.'

Mrs Nelligan clucked sympathetically. Such matrimonial tales of discardment were not unknown to her, coming from a country where the male flit to Britain was the natives' sole recognition of what constituted procedures of a divorce.

'Perhaps you will be more fortunate next time,' she murmured as Ms Maguire ushered her into Mr Donelli's office, where Torch presided, wrapped around by a massive mahogany desk whose surface was untouched by anything as untidy as working documents, blotters, or the little trappings of a business executive. There was an enormous green glass ashtray, the regulation photograph of a rather sour-looking matron with a lush-looking young woman alongside her, who gave promise of following in her mother's footsteps along the indulgent road to overweight when she got to her twenties. Torch, who didn't really like his daughter over much and his wife not at all, kept the picture he really enjoyed looking at in the locked middle drawer of his desk. But since it was a nude photograph of his current girlfriend, a high-class go-go dancer named Laurie Mae, he couldn't very well exhibit such charms in public on the top of his desk. Anyway, people would really think Laurie Mae had put her jewelled ear muffs in the wrong spots should they be privileged to study the photo in detail and Torch wasn't going to have them think Laurie Mae was dumb. He almost loved Laurie Mae when he thought about it.

He was quite curious as to what was bringing Mrs Nelligan along to see him. Because he simply could not believe that her visit was purely a social one. In Torch's experience any visiting tourist, with or without financial resources, usually wanted something from the Associates when they stopped by the building. Sometimes it was the fare home, sometimes it was a donation to one of the native charities, often it was a political visit, or in some cases a firm demand for assistance in dealing with leaners in the commercial opposition – but social calls were few and far between.

And he rarely felt called upon to produce refreshments of any kind for his visitors, who he thought were getting enough consideration by having their requests more or less granted on demand (at a price, it is true). Consequently, he was quite nonplussed when his receptionist – the available-for-matrimony-again Ms Maguire – appeared in his office doorway bearing a neatly laid tray with teapot, teabags, and even hot and cold milk just in case Mrs Nelligan drank her afternoon brew with warmed up cow juice. Which was, Mrs Nelligan told Katie later, extremely kindly meant.

Mrs Nelligan removed her white gloves. 'Shall I pour?' she asked gently. Without waiting for an answer, she handed Torch a cup of tea adding two spoons of sugar, since she had always found men to have a sweet tooth. (Torch couldn't stand the taste of sugar in anything, preferring a dollop of bourbon in his cup and then only if the said cup contained good strong Java. Tea, he believed, should be left to the Chinese to imbibe. But such was Mrs Nelligan's effect on him that he obediently accepted the cup and actually endeavoured to drink the contents without grimacing.)

'I am so delighted to actually meet the President of the Associates of American Democracy, face to face. We hear quite a good deal about the Society and its affiliations with the Friendly Sons of Saint Brigid, back home in Ireland, at regular intervals,' she said, fluttering her eyelashes at a bemused Torch.

'Oh – yeah – we do lotsa good things for the Irisha in America,' said Torch defensively. After all, one never knew who had sent this haybag along; it could even be a test from the Godfathers to see if he was handling things properly. 'Anda of course, we helpa the Italiani as well when they comea over here froma the olda country,' he added hastily.

'You are no doubt aware of my ambitions for my village back in Ireland,' continued Mrs Nelligan. 'I expect you have seen the publicity on the television. Personally, I don't read the newspapers very much myself any more. All one gets is doom and gloom these days – financial crises, unemployment – the good news is scarce, which is probably why the little story about Hackstown received so much coverage.'

Torch nodded, still not quite sure how to take his visitor. She smiled brightly at him and produced an envelope from her handbag.

'America has been extremely kind in its contributions to make Hackstown into a prosperous tourist venue,' she said. 'I feel it would be quite wrong to take all those contributions back to Ireland without making some gesture of thanks to your country. So I have decided that a cheque to the

Associates of American Democracy to fund a scholarship for a promising young Irish emigrant to go to Harvard Business school would be quite appropriate. I feel confident that the Associates will match the amount dollar for dollar?'

Torch blinked, struck silent not only by her words, but by a certain unworthy thought that either the Associates or the Friendly Sons of St Brigid were being set up somewhere along the line. But then, he reasoned, how in hell could this old bat have gained the inside track of the newspaper articles he had had published on the instructions of the Familia, (after he leaned on Jamesey Quilligan of course). Wasn't she almost a total stranger to American methods of discrediting the competition, and hadn't she as good as told him she never read the morning broadsheets anyhow? So he smiled widely, his diamond-studded left incisor glittering in the brightness of the office neon lighting, and he casually held out a beefy hand to receive Mrs. Nelligan's sizeable cheque. Any ideas he may have had about appropriating the money quietly on behalf of his employers was quashed when, two days later, he was cornered into turning up on television with Daniel, and was obliged publicly to commit the Associates to meeting the face amount on the cheque for the scholarship foundation. Only his quick-wittedness in offering a job to the first graduate ensured that, for the first term of the scholarship at least, the Mafia would get themselves a qualified accountant chosen from their own ranks, trained and paid for by the charity of the American public. And though they saw through the ploy, Daniel and Mrs Nelligan decided it was a small price to pay for hoisting the Familia, just for once. The business part of her visit now safely concluded, Agnes had time for conversation.

'You know, Mr Donelli,' she began, 'genealogy is one of my interests. Are you aware, for example, that many of the Italian families of today are descendants of the Irish Wild Geese, the rebels who fled my country to fight for other lands? The O'Donnells, the O'Mahoneys, the O'Neills – they had to leave Ireland to avoid being put to death by the invading forces of England some centuries back.'

Torch stared at her in puzzlement. He couldn't quite fathom what she was on about, history never having been his strong point during the few short years he was obliged to spend in the educational deserts of Little Italy.

Mrs Nelligan nodded, her curls bobbing gently. 'You know, Mr Donelli, I would not be at all surprised if back in your own family you came from one of the great O'Neill families, who may originally have settled in France before moving to Italy. The "D" in front of your name would possibly have been used to indicate the family as being "de" or "of" the O'Neills, hence Donelli. Yes, I would say it is more than probable that your forebears were of the distinguished O'Neill family.' She looked carefully into the middle distance.

Now slow on the uptake, Torch was not, and the entire situation clicked suddenly into perspective for him.

'You tryin' to tella me I mighta not be Italiano at all?' he asked.

'Good gracious me, no,' protested Mrs Nelligan. 'I merely suggest that your ancestors, while settling in Italy, and over a generation or so, could have Italianised the name through the French and Irish derivations. Historically, your forebears may well have been part of what is termed "The Flight of the Earls". You can most likely claim solid Irish roots to your family tree, Mr Donelli,' and she smiled her most innocently guileless smile at the mesmerised Torch.

Now it was established fact among the New York guardians of the city's law and order, peace and security, that Mr Pius 'Torch' Donelli was an unwelcome immigrant, who, if it could be arranged by any legal method at all, would greatly enhance the city by his permanent absence from its environs, preferably by a departure back to his native Sicily. They were even prepared to stand him the fare home, if they could persuade him to leave, but so far Torch had outwitted them on every count. Now he suddenly realised that while deportations of Italian troublemakers was quite a regular affair, the return of an Irish prodigal was infinitely more rare. Therefore to be in a position to claim Irish citizenship would almost certainly cement his chances of remaining in the Land of Opportunity on a permanent basis, free from official hassling, blessed by the Irish American *entente cordiale*.

For Torch, it was immediately a happy day. His diamond-studded tooth shone brighter than ever; he buzzed Ms Maguire and told her to break out the drinks cupboard, insisting, without brooking a refusal, on pouring Mrs Nelligan a double schooner of his finest sherry. Initially, he was about to press a treble measure of Irish whiskey into her white gloved hand, but was hastily advised against it by his secretary, whose finer instincts appreciated that a gentlewoman like Agnes would never touch the produce of the grain; Agnes was definitely a grape person, Ms Maguire accurately surmised.

Torch was well up on the details of citizenship, single and dual, and it took him no length of time at all, the following day, to contact a couple of minions in the appropriate departments to have his papers suitably re-administered, much to the chagrin of the New York police, who had now lost all possibilities of transferring Mr Donelli to the loving care and attention of the Italian guardians of the law. For the Family, of course, it was a choice between the annexation of the Hackstown fund or the eventual deportation of one of their more useful branch leaders, so they settled for what they had, and hoped that eventually they might manage to install a gambling casino in the Hackstown complex to compensate them for losing the manipulation of what the more irreverent members of the media were already calling the 'Leprechaun's Loot'.

The next edition of the newspapers carried laudatory articles on the Investathon and fervent disclaimers of the cruel and untrue rumours they had misguidedly printed the previous day, blaming the Communists for the whole thing.

It was most heartening to see how enthusiastic Mr Donelli became at further fund raising on the East Side after Daniel had co-opted him onto the Administration Committee. Torch organised one of the more prestigious cultural events, a concert of operatic works from leading Italian singers working throughout America, all donating their services free. And if he skimmed two per cent off the top from the amount the event finally raised, it was, one had to admit, a percentage very much below the Mafia's usual going rate.

Chapter Eleven

Mrs Nelligan's flight back from New York was quite uneventful. She was more than a little sad leaving Katie, whose brightness she knew she would miss around the apartment, when she returned to her own little cottage in Hackstown. Indeed, she had grown quite attached to the aroma of coffee at breakfast time, even if she resolutely refused to drink it first thing in the morning. And surprisingly, she found herself missing Daniel more than a little. Mr Hogan's interests were far flung, almost as wide as her own in fact, and they had spent a good deal of time discussing an infinite variety of subjects together while Agnes was in New York. One of the things she greatly missed in Hackstown village, worthy and all as the natives might be, was a certain level of intellectual stimulation which, over her academic years, she had grown used to enjoying.

But there was work to be done, and it was high time she ended what had started off as her annual holiday. Now she had to present the Hackstown village leaders with what was somewhat of a *fait accompli*, and she wasn't quite sure how they would accept what she had arranged. On the flight home, she devoted her attentions to the best method of selling the idea of a complex, and was toying with a few alternatives when her plane landed at Dublin airport.

She was more than surprised to find herself ushered off the aircraft with considerable ceremony and conducted into one of the VIP lounges where there was quite a gathering, all, it seemed, intent on greeting her with more than a modicum of respect and excitement. Mrs Nelligan found she was suddenly holding not only a press conference but a sort of political audience since the Minister for Leisure and

Affiliated Arts was actually present and about to present her with a bouquet of flowers as well! His assistant, she saw, was one of her old boys, and as she shook an admonishing finger at him, he hurried over to her.

'We've all been reading the newspaper stories from America about your efforts to save Hackstown, and of course we had newscasts on television too,' he explained. 'All the media crowd are mad to get the story from you first hand, and the Minister is most interested in the project.'

'I can imagine,' said Mrs Nelligan drily.

'Of course, he had something similar in mind . . .' Joseph glanced at her and then his voice trailed away as she stared him down. 'Well, someone would have thought of something, some day, I guess . . . you know I have to back the Minister, Mrs Nelligan.'

'Not,' said Mrs Nelligan with some asperity, 'to the extent of telling a falsehood so that your colleague can gain credit for something he had absolutely nothing to do with. Joseph, if politics is going to turn you into an untruthful lackey, perhaps you should find an alternative career!'

'Yes ma'am,' said Joseph shamefacedly. Then he brightened. 'At any rate, the Minister is delighted with the plan and he has every intention of helping you achieve it with the minimum of red tape – so it can't be all bad.'

Mrs Nelligan nodded, reserving her acceptance until she worked out what profit margin there might be in it for the Minister.

The newspaper reporters were most flattering. Mrs Nelligan was an ideal interviewee and she answered all their questions politely, with well-placed detail and colour, and gave them the statistics they dearly loved, plus enough big names to fill their columns with feature material for a week. The publicity preceded her down to Hackstown, where a welcoming committee awaited her in the square when she alighted from the Hackstown bus.

As the bus pulled into the square, she was almost deafened by the local brass and reed band, under the baton of the local schoolteacher, who, among his educational functions at the Mixed Infants, was also expected to teach the church junior choir and oversee the village brass and reed band whose members were prised from the Hackstown scout troop, somewhat unwillingly, as was now most obvious. He led the boys into a spirited but inaccurate rendering of 'O'Donnell Abu' which mercifully had to tail off in mid-note, as it were, when Mrs Nelligan dismounted and the bus pulled away again en route for the County Monaghan, where it hoped to deliver its four remaining passengers at an hour not estimated with any exactitude by either driver, conductor or the national transport system.

Its driver had long been known for the disregard he had for timetables and was quite content to take passengers who were interested in fishing to a quiet river he knew a bit off the regular route, if they happened to be angling enthusiasts. And if the weather was inclined to become inclement, then he would obligingly pull up somewhere along the way to Monaghan to allow his travellers to enjoy a leisurely meal. As he regularly declared, when the Lord made time he made plenty of it, and bus timetables neither did the actual driving nor sat in the seats until the destination was reached.

Agnes felt quite flattered as she observed the scene. There was Matt Quinlan with a tray on which sat an ice bucket with the top of a champagne bottle peering above it, plus a set of glasses, so obviously someone was going to propose a toast. That someone, she now discovered, was going to be Mr Charlie Donaghue, aided and supported by Mr Billy Markey, in his capacity as Honorary Secretary of the Golf Club, and more than likely the entrepreneur who would eventually be sorting out the zoning problems of the complex in his position of local auctioneer. Major Mulqueen, whose indignation was overridden by his determination not to be left out of anything in case he missed something, was standing as near to outside the welcoming group as he could decently manage without being mistaken for an onlooker.

Charlie darted forward, seizing Mrs Nelligan's hand in a bone-crushing grip, as he waved to the nearest young bandsman to get her luggage over to the hotel. Matt expertly popped the cork of the champagne bottle, poured her a glass and passed the rest around, carefully missing out the Major who was most disappointed since he had had great plans to refuse to drink the proposed toast, with all the hauteur he believed himself capable of.

Mrs Nelligan stood, looking her most bewildered and crushable, while Charlie eulogised on behalf of the citizens of Hackstown on her merits, her initiative, and her capabilities as a fundraiser supreme.

'There is no doubt, dear lady,' he boomed, 'that Hackstown will live to thank you every day of its existence for the prosperity you have ensured for the whole district where dependence on the unsupportable face of Capitalism will from now on be a thing of the past.'

The Major snorted. 'Goddamned rubbish! That complex is not going to come into existence, not even if the President of America comes over himself to build it.'

'And how do you propose to stop it?' Billy Markey asked truculently. 'You talk a lot of codology, do you know that, Mulqueen? The land isn't the Gun Club land any more; the President's wife is after donatin' it to the village. And takin' things all around as I find them, it mightn't be such a bad thing after all!'

'Oh to be sure it won't – for *you*,' sneered the Major under cover of the clapping which Mr Donaghue's well-meant if inaccurate statements had roused from the assembled Hackstown villagers. 'We all know you stand to get rich on the scheme. Not only will you do the land dealing but you'll profit from the construction side as well and God knows from how many other offshoots. Why should you be against it?'

'That's as may be,' admitted Billy without much regret. 'But if you play your cards right, you could cut yourself in for a piece of the financial action too. I mean, there must be some angle you can use to tighten the slack, and make yourself a crust or two at the same time.' And with a smile, Billy followed the party into the hotel, leaving the Major grinding his teeth while he stood alone in the suddenly deserted square where two small boys chasing a long-tailed brown mongrel dog were now the only signs of life.

Everyone was in the hotel lounge, drinking up a party, and it was regrettable that no one bothered to try and persuade the Major to climb down off his high horse and join in the celebrations. To tell the truth, no one was anxious to include him in the gathering, least of all Mrs Mulqueen, who was having a good time on large gins, which made a delightful change from the sweet brown sherry her husband insisted was what 'nice women' drank whether they liked it or not, and Mrs Mulqueen did not. Mrs Nelligan was regaling her with detailed information about the shopping in New York, and Katinka's boutique, in between explaining about the genealogical exactitude of her discoveries.

'We should have a little meeting tomorrow morning when we can review the situation,' she told Matt Quinlan quietly. 'We won't get much useful discussion going tonight.' It was to her credit that she remained steadfastly with the assembled company until the party ended somewhat noisily long past official closing time, when the Pearsons insisted on taking her to their home for a celebratory steak supper just to show their appreciation of the prosperous life she was about to bestow on the entire community as well as themselves.

Agnes settled down in her bed long after midnight, and if she blamed the steak for the restless sleep she had, in which her dreams featured Katie and Jonathan holding on to her arms, while Daniel was leaning over a locked gate waving her goodbye as she boarded a plane marked surprisingly with the name 'Heaven', then it shows that even headmistresses with initiative don't know exactly everything, particularly about themselves.

But she was extremely clear headed when she cycled into the forecourt of the Castle Court Hotel next morning, with a heavy briefcase firmly clipped to the carrier of her bike. Matt Quinlan hurried out and carried it to her usual table which he now augmented with a second table plus six seats. It was obvious that he was expecting the Major to swallow his temper and let his curiosity win the place at the committee meeting.

Major Mulqueen, followed by his not-so-loving wife, strutted into the lounge, straight to the counter and ordered a large Scotch and the usual sweet brown sherry. Mrs

Mulqueen shuddered her way into an adjacent chair, and cast an agonised glance at Matt, who gently placed a black coffee before her, accompanied by a couple of aspirin tablets. Hiding his arm carefully from the Major, he laced the coffee with a generous measure of Irish whiskey. 'Do you a power of good, ma'am, for what ails you,' he whispered, and poured the sherry quickly down the sink, replacing the nauseous liquid with more of the good ten-year-old he had added to her coffee cup. The Major failed to observe any of this, being much too concerned with finding some way to forget his umbrage so that he would be allowed to stay for the meeting and thus not miss anything important.

The Major had not been idle while the others were celebrating in the Castle Court the night before. He had marched home, followed, it must be said, by the brown mongrel dog who, having accompanied him to his front gate and been routed by the Major's walking stick, had slid behind him up the front drive and peed over his doorstep.

The Major had observed this performance with considerable annoyance, but being in the middle of the first of his telephone calls, he could do nothing about it. Two hours after his arrival back at his house, the Major had telephoned every influential name he could think of, going right back to his service days, names on all sides of the political divide and the results were not promising.

He found a surprising enthusiasm for the proposed Tir na n-Og complex in Hackstown among those he spoke with. His Labour party and trades union contacts were delighted that the problems of work and the financial provision of an industry for Hackstown would soon be off their agendas. The current party in government was expecting to make considerable political mileage from the project which its members had already convinced themselves was entirely of their doing. The Opposition party, believing that a general election was imminent, within a few months at most, decided it could use the complex as an example of the kind of high life their party's governing power could generate once they were handling the Irish economy. So Major Mulqueen found that protestors were not exactly beating a

112

path to the village to prevent the Gun Club from losing its shooting preserves. It would, he realised, have to be handled at local level by his own members. And they had responded to a man, he was glad to recall.

The perpetrators of this outrageous takeover would get a run for their money, he resolved, but in the meantime, it was important to know what they were planning if he and his associates were going to put an effective spoke in the wheels. So he greeted Mrs Nelligan with as much charm as he could muster, and insisted on buying her the customary sweet brown sherry which she left untouched on the counter, being sensibly convinced that a sweet brown sherry was a liquor one might occasionally cook with, but would never imbibe, and Matt removed the offending glass replacing it with Mrs Nelligan's own favourite dry pale Amontillado.

Geoffrey and Marjorie Pearson came armed with notepads, determined to start in a businesslike manner from the beginning. They knew from rather bitter experience that their previous efforts at making a possible killing hadn't been blessed with major success largely because Geoffrey had two faults which mitigated against him: he was extremely trusting of mankind and absolutely lousy at maths.

The Pearsons too had been busy while Mrs Nelligan was in New York. They had consulted with Geoffrey's brother Julian, with the architectural connections, and his friend Simon had paid a fleeting visit to the house and was even now busily drawing up plans to make a little conversion which would not take an arm and a leg from their funds to complete. Marjorie had also rung around her wide family circle and had firm promises of elegant junk which she could use to stock the shop once she conveyed it home and converted it into something usable. Geoffrey had spent profitable hours perusing the ancient deeds, maps and rights of way attached to the estate, and was more than elated to discover that the stream which fed the lake and ultimately provided water for the entire site, actually rose on his land and travelled quite a way through the estate before it arrived on the common land.

There was also the little matter of a major pathway

through the woodland which bordered the demesne, without access to which an additional five-mile trek would be added for the complex users, should Geoffrey decide to close off the fences. All in all, his time spent up in the attics of Hackstown House, amid the dust, the moth-eaten antlers, the suits of armour and mouldering leather-covered books, was more than well spent. Not that Geoffrey was about to throw any spanners in the works of the proposed complex, but he certainly intended to put a price on certain concessions, unless they could be negotiated for other favours which might be more valuable to him. His happiest thought was that at last he could get rid of those damned sheep. Thanks to an unexpected run of passable TV viewing reception from their ancient and temperamental television set, Geoffrey had caught a documentary on commercial deer raising and was now about to get out of mutton and into venison, which he hoped he would market to the tables of the new complex among other potential customers. And somehow, venison production sounded a more suitable occupation for a country gentleman than worming ewes.

Mrs Nelligan finally called the meeting to order when she had drunk her coffee and observed that Charlie Donaghue's colour had been restored to its usual puce tinge, once he had consumed his daily curer. As she took her seat at the top of the table, the company noticed she had slid an extra chair in beside her own, and they wondered who was going to use it. The Major made a move to occupy it, convinced that only he could be permitted co-chairmanship of such an important gathering. A steely look from Mrs Nelligan's bright blue eyes halted him in his tracks and he harumphed his way further down to another vacant seat.

The lounge door opened and a most elegant personage appeared. He was immaculately grey-suited with a pale mauve silk tie knotted at the collar of a lavender-tinted shirt. His shoes and socks matched each other exactly and he was barbered and manicured to a perfection that Hackstown could never hope to achieve without a weekly flight to one of London's best-known salons. Mrs Nelligan smiled delightedly at the vision.

'Do come in, Roger dear. I am so glad you managed to get

here at such short notice,' she trilled at him.

The young man, carrying a hide briefcase that cost enough to provide a two-week luxury holiday in the Bahamas, threw his arms around her and planted a smacking kiss on her rosy cheek.

'For you, dear Aunt Agnes, I would come half-way around the world – in fact I almost did. I was in Tokyo when my secretary telexed me that you needed some advice, so here I am.'

Mrs Nelligan introduced him. 'This is my nephew, Roger Nelligan. He is by way of being an entrepreneur and business consultant, and I felt he would be useful to advise us on a few little details.'

Roger nodded, took his place beside his aunt at the head of the table and produced a file of papers, a pad, and a gold pen with his initials picked out in brilliants down the barrel. Billy Markey envied him and resolved that the next good deal he closed, he would treat himself to a decent writing pen, tie-pin and pinkie ring, preferably one like Roger's which was a rather beautiful scarab ring in heavy gold. That, Billy told himself, had definite class.

Rapidly, Roger reviewed Mrs Nelligan's general plans for the complex, sorted out the many vissicitudes of permissions, subcontractions, contracts and leases. His contacts were legion, his grasp of what his aunt had in mind immediate and comprehensive and his imagination of considerable help in developing new ideas to enhance the current plans. The meeting was highly successful, and when Roger had finished giving his expert advice, Mrs Nelligan was more than a little encouraged by his enthusiastic projections not to mention the portfolio of suitable and willing investors he was able to produce, if the committee needed outside investment.

A quick meal at the hotel, and Roger whirled away back to town in his Porsche, promising to get things underway. Two days later, a group of well-heeled Japanese industrialists in Tokyo happily completed their designs, estimates and guarantees for the major construction contract of the complex, the residential section, which, as Mrs Nelligan decreed, was going to recreate the beehive huts of the ancient Celts. The idea was not alien to the industrialists, who had, a couple of years before, dispatched a quartet of their own architects to do a survey on the archeological megalithic remains of the County Meath, simply because they believed the same sort of buildings were common to both countries, and they were trying to find a way to make use of the design. Their stint was now about to pay off, and if the huts were to be constructed in plastic instead of clay and stone and wattles, at least when they began manufacture, they wouldn't be expected to pay 'dirty money' to the employees at the factory in Ireland for pouring polypropylene moulds. Progress, they felt, could sometimes replace ancient culture at a highly competitive level; after all, look at the automobile industry!

They telexed Roger and he negotiated a year's lease on the Hackstown plastics factory before the Americans realised the tender for the housing was up for grabs. The phallic mushroom-shaped stool moulds were replaced by beehive moulds which when cast were carefully painted to simulate the original finish as described by the archeologist whom Roger had sensibly hired as advisor to his Japanese clients, Mr Okami and his associates.

Mr Okami, a rotund little man with numerous grandchildren, when he paid a visit to Hackstown, was instantly enchanted with the whole place. He established an ancillary wing to the factory, in which ten Hackstown teenagers were gainfully employed making miniature replicas of the beehive huts, which, when opened in the middle, revealed a tiny leprechaun sitting on a spray of plastic shamrock. He did quite a spin-off trade exporting them to America later, in time for St Patrick's Day.

Chapter Twelve

It was only when a few weeks later the construction machinery, in all its red and yellow glory, moved on to the site, that the first of Major Mulqueen's moves against the complex went into operation.

When the excavator and digger and earth mover operators turned up for their first day's clearing work on the site, they found why the Gun Club committee had completed the run of barbed-wire fencing around the near perimeter of the club house. The entrance gate had been firmly wired up as well, and outside it, in what one might almost call 'serried ranks' was a determined-looking collection of hefty males, accompanied, it had to be assumed, by equally unprepossessing-looking wives, with tweed hats, business-like brogue shoes, blackthorn sticks, and woollen stockings. Each female of the species carried a satchel which obviously housed the spare boxes of cartridges belonging to the shotguns each male of the party was brandishing. Fifty of them lined up in military precision was a somewhat imtimidating sight, and understandably the little Japanese foreman who headed the ground clearance crew was not prepared to tangle with the natives who came armed with guns instead of cherry blossom. He smiled nervously at all and sundry in a highly ingratiating fashion, removing his yellow tin safety helmet and bowing endlessly as the Major approached him with a most belligerent expression.

'You gettum out of here, chop chop – no diggy uppy groundie,' the Major roared, firmly convinced that his own invention of what he believed was authentic pidgin English would do the trick.

The foreman bowed almost to shoe level and in

immaculate Oxfordian vernacular, he advised the Major that he had full permission to level the ground in advance of the construction crews. Major Mulqueen waved him away and prepared to make a speech to his assembled companions.

'I want to thank all of you for turning up here today to stage this protest which I also feel sure will win us our right in this matter!'

The Major was now into full spate, his bull neck swelling above his collar rather like the wattles of a turkey. He waved his own shotgun about in an alarming fashion so that the excavating crew instinctively dived for cover behind their vehicles, their experience in foreign lands having made them quick of reaction and instant at self-preservation when threatened by people waving guns in the air. The Major looked rather surprised for a moment, and then dismissed the scuffle from his mind.

'We will picket this side constantly from now on,' he stated loudly. 'Anyone who tries to build on this land will have to mow all of us down first. If it takes forever, we will maintain a twenty-four-hour picket at this gate. Let's see what the company trying to destroy the Hackstown Gun Club will do about that!'

The men began to look slightly harried as Major Mulqueen struck up an untuneful version of 'We Shall Overcome' joined by several of the tweed-hatted women in the front of the picket. It was clear that the males of the party had no wish to get sucked into a twenty-four-hour protest routine. After all, they had farms to run, businesses to prove profitable, and dinners, meetings and other forms of commercial occupation to attend to. A fair proportion of them eased themselves into the club house, from which, by the back entrance, they sidled out and into their automobiles once more, leaving only the committee standing firmly in the bar with a sizeable group of the women in attendance, most of them remaining more from curiosity than from conviction.

Grasping his glass under his chin, the Major stood, gazing, Napoleon-like, into middle distance through the club house window. The excavation crew were gathered around the little Japanese foreman, and from the group, distantly, on the morning air, a growing rumble was beginning to emanate. He smiled in satisfaction; any minute now, he told himself, the crew would walk off the site in support of the picket line, in true union solidarity.

It shocked him considerably to observe that after a handshake between the foreman and the workmen, the yellow-helmeted excavation crew raced for their machines, and with an almighty roar, started up their engines. Major Mulqueen rounded on his side-kick, a meek little man retired from the Civil Service where he had pursued a totally undistinguished career in the Taxation department, and ordered him to go and see what was going on. The little man raced away and returned as quickly.

'The foreman says the picket is not an official trades union picket and as such has no standing where his operatives are concerned. Added to which, he has just offered them a bonus if they stay on the job,' he told the Major, blinking nervously and looking as if he were prepared to duck rapidly should the Major suddenly lose control of his temper.

'How can a damn foreman have the authority to offer bonuses? That's management's decision,' spluttered Major Mulqueen, banging his glass down on the bar counter.

'Because he *is* the management: his uncle is head of the construction consortium,' replied the little tax inspector sadly, grasping thankfully at the cup of coffee one of the tweedy ladies passed to him over the counter.

'My God – that does it! To think we have Nips running the business of this country. I always said that the Development Authority was selling this country to the highest bidder and paying them to come and take it over, to boot!' The Major banged his tumbler with a teaspoon, to engage the attentions of his supporters, now down to a mere fifteen or so. Two of the ladies had had to go home to attend the Countrywomen's committee meeting. They all sat down obediently, leaving the Major standing in front of the bar.

'I want every bit of farm machinery and every automobile you have between you lined up this lane tomorrow morning so that we block off the entrance to the site. Meantime, I will demand a meeting with the "Hackstown leisure complex committee", as they call themselves, so that we can put our demands and ultimatums to them immediately.'

'I don't think that we have a leg to stand on,' remarked one man. 'The only thing left to us is to negotiate for some concessions, Oliver. We never owned the land, and now the leisure complex committee holds official title.'

'Possession is nine-tenths of the law,' replied the Major firmly. 'If we're here, they can't move in to do anything until they shift us. When the rest of the Irish gun clubs see the siege we'll be under, they'll surely come down and help us out. Public opinion is a very strong motivator – and the gun clubs have a lot of clout.' The Major spoke more from hope than from actual belief. 'Maybe if we can delay things long enough they'll come up with another scheme to use the money from America and we'll get the land back again. Anyway, we've just begun to fight. They haven't seen anything yet. I have a few ideas up my sleeve to make life difficult for them.'

The complex committee was more than willing to meet the Gun Club supporters. In fact, Mrs Nelligan had already planned for the occasion.

The meeting of the two factions had been arranged to take place on the neutral ground of the Parish Hall which was slightly off-putting for the Major, since the Hall did not boast of a dispense bar. Matt Quinlan, being on the leisure complex committee, felt it would be inopportune to hold any gathering connected with what might ultimately prove to be a confrontation situation on his hotel premises, in case it could be said he stood to profit from the refreshments which would be sold. Anyway, he quite enjoyed watching Major Mulqueen suffer from alcoholic deprivation, whenever possible.

The meeting began badly, thanks to Major Mulqueen's pigheaded insistence on the blockage of the lane leading on to the Gun Club lands. The leisure complex committee was very tight-lipped when it filed in and sat around the table in the Parish Hall.

'We'll get nowhere until you clear the laneway and let the

construction crew in to do their work,' Billy Markey said loudly.

Major Mulqueen looked innocent. 'Clear the lane, Billy? What is blocking the lane, may I ask?'

Billy scowled at him. 'You know damn well that the tractors and haybalers and cabs belonging to a score or more of your members are packed tit to tail in the lane, so don't try to deny it!'

The Major raised his eyebrows. 'Oh *that*? We promised our members some time ago to provide a free engine check for all their farm vehicles. One of our members has a leading heavy machinery engineer over to his factory from America, and he said he would bring him down for a couple of days' shooting, and at the same time get him to do a complimentary check-over for other members, on their farm machinery. You know what importance the Department of Agriculture sets on safety checks of farm equipment. It's unfortunate that the visit should coincide with the start of your excavation work, isn't it? But the club area was the ideal spot for all the machinery to be collected at the same time.'

'Well,' gritted Billy, 'If your members don't shift their machinery today, they'll find there won't be either an engine part or a drum of diesel available to them from my store next time they have need of it, and I could also delay ordering a few other items like feeding stuffs and seed potatoes. Now that might cause as much of an upset as the block up in the lane is doing right now.'

There was a low murmur and several figures moved swiftly out of the Parish Hall. Mrs Nelligan smiled at the group still remaining.

'I am sure you have all given the subject some thought as we have ourselves, and we realise that some form of compensation would be compatible until your club is relocated. Since the local people are forming a co-operative movement to invest in the complex, with preferential treatment for the co-operative members when the ancilliary services are being dispensed, we thought if we gave Hackstown Gun Club two hundred and fifty extra shares as

121

a gift, plus a lump sum for the club house building, it would be acceptable.'

A stocky farmer in a bright yellow waistcoat over well-worn jodhpurs suddenly rose to his feet. He had a small coterie around him and it was clear they had taken a firm commercial look at what was being set up.

'We'll be looking for a deal more than that, ma'am,' he said loudly. 'We reckon we ought to have all the shooting rights and the fishing rights so that we can sell licences to the tourists. We'd also be looking for the franchise to sell all the sportin' equipment, and we think we ought to be the ones to operate the boats on the lake. And we'd want to set up a good clay-pigeon range that we could operate on commercial lines.' He sat down amid a murmur of agreement, not to say several cheers from his companions. The Major leaped to his feet, incensed at the perfidious treachery from within his own band.

'Are you prepared to sell out Hackstown Gun Club for a paltry cash return?' he roared at the stocky man who nodded back at him calmly.

'Oliver, I told you yesterday that you'd have to accept the facts. How can we buck the President of the United States? So why not take what we can get and make something out of it? Times are hard.'

'Never!' shouted Major Mulqueen, glancing frantically around at his own immediate supporters. His followers instinctively closed in around him while the stocky man mustered his group to his side. Clearly the Gun Club was going to be split. Mrs Nelligan blinked her blue eyes at all of them.

'There now,' she said happily. 'I knew we would all come to an amicable agreement once we talked things over. My committee will certainly discuss the points you have raised and I am sure we will come to an arrangement which will be agreeable to all of us.' And she gathered up her folders, pen and handbag, smiled brilliantly at the gathering and betook herself out of the hall, escorted by Matt Quinlan and followed by the rest of the committee who were quite lost in admiration at her summary wrap up of the Gun Club protestors.

Back at the hotel, they reached a swift decision on the demands of the stocky man and his colleagues, negative on the shooting and fishing rights – already promised to Geoffrey who had agreed to organise small deer hunts on his land as long as the tourists agreed not to slaughter the herd, and since he owned the main section of the trout stream, it being on his land, then it was only fair he should get the fishing franchise too – but they could have the clay-pigeon range and the sporting goods franchise too. And if they agreed to build a boat repair yard and a small marina on the upper end of the lake away from the tourist traffic, then they could look after the boating facilities. By the time the Gun Club members had carved up the business amongst themselves, Mrs Nelligan felt they would not find much to protest about, apart from the Major of course. He, she could see, would not be placated, not because he was unaffected by the thoughts of future prosperity for himself and his lady wife, but simply because he had obviously now painted himself into a corner and could not find a way out which would not land either a hand or a foot in the high gloss.

The idea of forming a village co-operative had, after a doubtful start, mostly on the part of the farmers in the outlying district who viewed any shared effort with the utmost suspicion, got off the ground in a satisfactory manner. It was being run most efficiently by the bookkeeper who had once headed the accounts department of the departed plastics factory, a young woman named Kitty Dermody, who was more than pleased to be re-employed, particularly when she had found a useful deposit for her redundancy payment and was able to keep a careful eye on her capital at the same time. Her undoubted charm and her reputation for total honesty, efficiency and financial expertise, induced the most cautious of her ex-workmates to put their money where it would, as she told them firmly, do them the most good. Once the factory staff came across, they spread the word among friends and family, all of whom promptly raided mattresses, piggy-banks and post-office savings, which caused quite a run on the local office savings for a week or more. Miss Dermody issued weekly balance sheets and neat little record books, and with some forethought, she turned her front room into an office and set herself up as a registered company. Once she got the co-operative off the ground, she turned her attentions to the finance houses and building societies, who were quite pleased to allow her to operate on their behalf in Hackstown – and Kitty became one of the initial success stories that made such good television copy for the States when, later on, Ambrose Carter sent his units from WCTTI to immortalise the new complex for American posterity.

Now, if Matt Quinlan's only son, who had betaken himself to Dublin to study hotel management, hadn't got himself involved with a university student named Lizzie Carter, who was trying not to get too deeply immersed in the subject of archeology in Trinity College, life might have taken a very different turn in Hackstown's Castle Court Hotel.

Gerald Quinlan was a most correct young man who was determined to prove to his father that handing over the Castle Court Hotel to him once he completed his management course was the soundest move Matt would ever make. He had met Lizzie when she and four male companions tried to gatecrash a Press Reception at the hotel in which Gerald was serving his time until he revitalised the commercial world of the Castle Court Hotel. Lizzie was totally tactless, fearless, very independent, free-thinking and very beautiful, and Gerald fell madly in love with her. He promptly ejected her companions, and settled Lizzie in a corner with a glass of champagne from which she was salvaged by a somewhat precious-looking photographer who snapped her with the party host and made her instantly famous as a setter of new fashion. Lizzie had turned out in a home-made ribbon dress made from strips of coloured cotton mounted on a knitted yoke, under which she was keeping her splendid limbs beautifully warm with a pair of granddad combinations dyed a vivid scarlet. Lizzie still attended archeology lectures in between any modelling sessions she could be bothered to accept bookings for, but for some unknown reason, she always kept her dates with Gerald. She called him her Luck Penny, and actually got a real penny gold-dipped and put on a chain for him to wear around his neck. It says much for the effect she had on him that Gerald wore it constantly, since he had the Irish rural male's contempt for anything that smacked of urban sissiness.

It was Lizzie who, idly tracing back some of the local archeological remains of Hackstown in the College Library one day, discovered that a long-departed early castle on the site of the Castle Court Hotel had a couple of dungeons wherein the ungodly were incarcerated and worked upon long enough to convert them into most upright folk. This was news to Gerald and would no doubt be a revelation to his father. Gerald felt that if the dungeons could be located and opened up, there might be a new niche for an enterprising young assistant hotel manager to get involved in – such as a disco with a medieval torture chamber theme. Gerald could see it all: waiters dressed up like executioners, with masks and hoods, chains and whips hanging from the walls; old instruments and implements of historic inhumanity for decor and horrific sounds of anguish in stereo; not to speak of continuously running videos depicting the sort of medieval mind-bending the history books glossed over so neatly. Lizzie thought it was a marvellous notion and proposed a dungeon hunt for the earliest possible date she could muster up enough associates to accompany them to Hackstown.

Gerald, torn between his ambitions and his anxiety as to what his parents might think of his beautiful Lizzie and her somewhat unusual friends, was swept along with her enthusiasm, and before he knew it was committed to bringing twenty individuals down to the hotel the following weekend to hunt for the dungeons, aided by some surprisingly competent-looking reconstruction drawings of the entire site provided by Lizzie. And Lizzie amazed Gerald even more by proving to be an excellent hand at pulling a pint in his father's lounge bar, which, even if he had not already fallen for her looks and her sweetness of manner, would have endeared her to Matt who had resigned himself years ago to the fact that Mrs Quinlan's talents lay in the culinary field and not in the world of the vintners. He was more than willing for Lizzie to go burrowing in the cellars of the hotel, but it was actually one of her companions, an earnest young woman named Emily, who discovered the stone slab with the remains of an iron pull-ring, almost buried beneath the turf stack in the corner of the hotel's rear courtyard which Matt's patrons usually used as an extra car parking area whenever the hotel was catering for a local wedding. It took a day for them to lever up the slab, but Lizzie felt it was worth it, when they found a flight of steps leading down to a subterranean cavern which opened into four other smaller areas. Gerald triumphantly explained his plans to his father, assisted by an enthusiastic Lizzie who promised Matt there would a regular stream of patrons to the most unusual disco in Ireland, an occurrence she would personally see to.

'She knows just about everybody,' said Gerald proudly, and Matt, still slightly confused, consented to the conversion, which, he warned Gerald, would have to pay its own way, independently of the hotel. Matt would be doing his own thing commercially, and would not be in a position to underwrite a failed disco.

It seemed a natural progression of affairs then, for the group to remain on in Hackstown to help Gerald and Lizzie get the disco organised. Anyway, the weather was super, Lizzie said, and they all adored camping out, once Gerald organised their meals at the hotel. They made quite good progress on the conversion, though Gerald devoutly hoped his father was unfamiliar with the smell of the content matter in their cigarettes, and he prayed nightly that his mother would not take it into her head to pay any social calls to the tents the students were occupying, without reasonable advance notice of her plans.

He and Lizzie went scouting around the district searching for the disco decor items, and Lizzie displayed unexpected talent for converting many innocent-looking ancient farmyard implements into horrendous looking instruments of torture. They found an old saddle-maker who made up several knotted-leather whips and binding thongs, and it was surprising how effective old rusted gin traps and poachers' snares looked when Lizzie painted them with luminous paint so that they would glow menacingly in the gloom of the dungeon rooms. It was amazing, too, how effective a couple of coats of white limewash could look on the old cellar walls, and the seating areas needed no more than woven rush matting around the rough wooden tables which Gerald had had thrown together by a local forestry worker.

All in all, Gerald had high hopes for the Dungeon Disco, and he awaited the completion of the leisure complex with impatience, commuting between his course in Dublin and Hackstown, where Lizzie and her friends still resided, a few of whom had actually managed to find employment on the leisure complex site, which money served to support the entire party quite comfortably. And since it was difficult to sort them out individually, they quietly established a rota working system among themselves which functioned admirably on the building site. Gerald worried about Lizzie down in Hackstown, but when he nervously asked her to marry him, she howled with laughter and kissing his cheek maternally, advised him to remember that two lived twice as expensively as one, and anyway, bits of paper got lost very easily. Meantime she had made friends with Mrs Nelligan, and was currently engaged in writing a definitive history of Hackstown and its archeological interests which Mrs Nelligan proposed to sell in the gift shop on the complex once Lizzie had the book completed.

Lizzie, Mrs Nelligan felt, would be quite an asset to the commercial life of the village, and she sincerely hoped that she would remain in Hackstown preferably for good. Agnes decided she would devote some attention to achieving this pious wish, once she got the Tir na n-Og going ahead on a more even keel. Had Gerald known Mrs Nelligan's intentions, he would no longer have felt it necessary to spend a small fortune in telephone calls to the Castle Court Hotel, reassuring himself that Lizzie had not taken it into her lovely head to go away with some exciting sophisticate and leave him to die of a broken heart in the bowels of the Dungeon Disco.

Chapter Thirteen

In the months that followed, it was surprising how motivated Hackstown became. It was quite a hive of activities of one kind or another.

There was a big run on the local library for books on Celtic mythology, ancient Ireland, archeological remains and fairy tales of all kinds, and Con Doolin the postman got very knowledgeable indeed about the various governmental departments being pressed into dispatching all kinds of information which the citizens of Hackstown thought might be of assistance to their plans. Regular bus-loads and association groups took themselves to the city to visit museums and collections and exhibitions of one sort or another. In fact, there was quite a stir at the National Museum where one of the co-op members in a display of over-enthusiasm went to take the bronze necklets dug up on the Viking site from their display cases to examine them more closely with a view to doing a reproduction job for the gift shop. Fortunately, Charlie Donaghue was in the party and his membership of the government circles was valuable in having the unthinking one released by the museum guards, when apologies had to be offered, along with assurances that the party wasn't trying to nick the ancient artefacts.

Hackstown was into ancient Irish culture up to its eyeballs. A Dublin theatrical school had opened a branch in the village so that those about to be involved in playing the parts of ancient Gaelic warriors, soldiers of Cuchulain and Finn McCool, Vikings, vassals of Queen Maeve, or chariot drivers for Deirdre of the Sorrows, when the Complex got into production, would at least know which end of their equipment was which.

Mr Okami of the Japanese consortium was already in the throes of buying a house in Hackstown. He kept finding new ideas to put into production – like the replicas of the Sword of Finn McCool which he planned to bury most carefully around the district so that the tourists could dig them up again. He was into ride-along plastic swans with little gold plastic crowns on their heads (he had read all about the Children of Lir who had been turned into swans and the legend fascinated him considerably). In fact he had added a refinement of his own: a marine model of the swans came equipped with a little pedal arrangement like the European pedalo craft, so his swans could swim in the waters of Lough Bawn, with a couple of passengers installed. He was also negotiating with a troupe of Japanese aquatic performers to come and stay for the season and give daily water-ballet shows on the lake, dressed up in swan costumes. He was into swanology in a big way, was Mr Okami. And he was turning out little mini-chariots for the children's play centre, which would be pulled by Shetland ponies which a horse trader in Co Monaghan was training for him.

While he was not intending to live in the house he was buying, since business back in Japan needed his constant attention, Mr Okami reckoned that his Number Two son was about ready to slip the parental tie and come out into the world of commerce in another country. Mr Okami felt that Hackstown would be a safe and educationally worthwhile project for young Li-San to cut his managerial teeth on, and, after all, his cousin who was supervising the construction operation would keep an eye on him. Which was where his calculations were inaccurate. Li-San hid an ambition to become a Samurai under his decorous black suit and blue shirt and when he watched the battles of the Fir Bolg being re-enacted later, in the complex, he joined the acting school in the village, and never again looked at a factory production line. He had, in time, however, a full and happy life touring the provinces of Ireland with his own fit-up company when being a stage warrior lost its initial charm, and he staged dramas ranging from O'Casey to Ibsen, and from the Red Barn to Japanese Kabuki.

There were villagers gainfully engaged in making up costumes for the personnel of Tir na n-Og – this was one contract Mrs Nelligan felt should not go to an outsider. You couldn't buy a used inner tube from a car, for love or money – someone had discovered a way to mould them into swords for the fighting soldiery – and a group of senior students at the secondary school in the village was about to become a Youth Employment Project success story when it went into production of shields and breastplates made from pâpier maché, the newspapers for which the group collected weekly from the entire district and recycled in a disused cottage which the students had converted into a workshop. There were people making up chain mail from chicken wire, women's groups crocheting madly every hour God sent, to stock the gift shop and dress the minstrels and the handmaidens in Celtic embroidered uniforms and suitable garments for the various historic events planned. A group was doing a crash course in medieval food preparation with a view to taking over a local castle in which to run medieval banquets at the weekends.

Mrs Nelligan was quite proud of them all.

'You know,' she said one morning to Matt as she was having her usual cup of coffee. 'The Opening will have to be of special importance. We need to do something quite outstanding to mark the occasion.'

'I'd have thought that Mrs President would come over herself for the affair – after all, it's her land,' said Matt thoughtfully.

'Well, yes, but I understand the Presidential election campaign will be well into its stride at the time and I cannot see Mrs Randolph leaving her husband's side just to come and declare a leisure complex open,' said Mrs Nelligan. Actually, she was not over-keen to play hostess to the First Lady since she was well aware that Hackstown would not figure in any plans which might be made for the occasion. The powers that were would certainly take over the visit of such an august personage, and the resulting chaos would take all the impact away from the Hackstown leisure complex. After all, since the village, the committee and Mrs

Nelligan herself had gone through a great deal to achieve it, there was no way they should lose out on the end product. Agnes hoped that her letter to the First Lady giving her ample room to back out of the official opening, would be answered by a missive full of good wishes and deep regrets at having to miss the occasion. She had an infinitely more interesting Personality in view to perform the ceremonies that would give a commercial Fairyland to tourism.

Mid-afternoon, when the lounge of the Castle Court Hotel was at its most deserted, Mrs Nelligan sat quietly in a corner with Matt, the Pearsons and Billy Markey, while she put her idea for Opening Day to her working committee.

'I presume, like myself, you are a little out of touch with the sort of music enjoyed by modern youth today?' she began, as she opened her familiar black notebook.

Geoffrey bristled just slightly – he was at an age when he was sensitive to being reminded what the date on his birth certificate really was.

'Oh, I would not say that, dear Mrs Nelligan. I like to keep in touch – Frank Sinatra, Bill Haley and all that,' he smiled with careful boyishness around the table.

His wife shook her head at him. 'No dear,' she sighed. 'They were *our* time. Mrs Nelligan is probably speaking of current teenage idols, the Jacksons, the Princes, the Ritchies ...'

Her husband stared at her in some puzzlement.

'They sound like a range of kitchen stoves,' he said sulkily, 'and I've never heard of any of them.'

Mrs Nelligan waited patiently until the exchange was over. 'We are speaking of that particular group of young luminaries, Marjorie, it is true,' she said. 'Believe me, I would not be as well-informed as your good self, had I not had one of its best-known members for a couple of terms when he was merely a gifted amateur on the percussion instruments of the school orchestra. Later of course, he took up singing for which, I regret to recall, he has little real talent, but for which he is now remarkably famous. And of course, he composes music, and is, I may say, one of the most highly paid entertainers in the world today.' She looked at her companions with no little satisfaction. 'On my school register, he was Jonas Bowman. You probably know him better as "Longbow".'

Even Geoffrey was awed into silence. 'Longbow' was so big it did not bear thinking about. He counted his following in millions, his wealth in billions. He was quite simply a living legend and such a megastar in the pop world, that he no longer was allowed to appear at public venues. In order to have a place in New York to live where he could not be got at, Longbow had to buy the entire twenty-five storey building so that he could set up home in the penthouse. He had a full staff of security guards who lived in apartments in the lower section of the building. He had a menagerie, an indoor jumping and exercise enclosure for his riding horses, minor refinements like a cinema, an Olympic-sized swimming pool, a solarium, a simulated stretch of beach in the basement which had a wave-making machine to make him imagine he was actually by a real sea, and because he didn't like to drink at home, there was a replica of an Olde English Coaching Inn, complete with wax figures of patrons, to which he could repair if he wanted a beer before dinner. And according to his last communication with his ex-headmistress, Longbow was bored to death and in need of a little stimulation. Which was why, he told her in his letter, any little thing he could do for her to move things along at Hackstown's proposed Tir na n-Og, news of which he had of course seen on TV, would be a welcome diversion.

'I thought,' said Mrs Nelligan casually, 'I might suggest to Jonas that he would fly over on a private visit to me, and at the same time, he could open the complex officially for us. What do you think of my idea?'

Her audience was totally dumbstruck. The publicity potential was instantly obvious. The financial input of such a public appearance would be immeasurable. But so would the crowds. Billy had a dreadful feeling that Hackstown would not be able to cope. He said as much, with infinite reluctance, since the last thing he wanted to do was to be a party to cancelling this marvel.

'Well now,' said Mrs Nelligan, 'I understand that Jonas has his own security staff, but I feel that the best way to ensure there would be no problems among either the local population or the fans who will undoubtedly congregate to see him, would be if we formed a protection corps of all the local teenagers in the area, and invited representatives of the Irish fan clubs to act as stewards as well. That way we would have a more co-operative atmosphere than if we allowed a commercial concern to do the policing for us. I have always found in my teaching career, that if you wanted a real organisational arrangement to succeed, then the people to put in charge of running it were the dissenters and the rebels – it worked like a charm every time. And of course, the responsibility was so good for their character formation too.' And she turned her most innocent smile on all of them.

'I can't see you getting a licence to allow him to perform at the complex,' said Billy, who had some little experience with running things like charity concerts, golf club dances and the odd celebrity gig. 'He's far too big, you know.'

Mrs Nelligan looked suitably shocked. 'Good gracious! Jonas will not be coming as a professional performer; this would be entirely a private visit on his part. The fact that he will be quite obviously pursued by enthusiasts of his particular musical influences, will be quite accidental. Of course, the local business community will obviously benefit from the occasion, for which I know Jonas will be more than delighted. He is well aware of the straits in which the village finds itself. Jonas was always a generous boy – he never grudged his time when it came to helping out at charity functions, Old Folks' entertainments or Open Days for the Orphanage, as I recall,' said Mrs Nelligan firmly.

Matt look disappointed. He had had sudden exciting visions of a hotel and lounge overflowing to capacity and was actually considering having the amplification brought up to standard on the small lounge stage.

Mrs Nelligan glanced at him from under lowered lashes. She smiled at him.

'Jonas will, of course, spend the nights at my house, but I felt I would like to have a dinner here for him as a little thank you. We would be about thirty or so, including the committee. I would leave all the arrangements to you and dear Mrs Quinlan, of course. Perhaps, however, you would arrange to have the piano in tune – Jonas does so dislike an instrument which is off-key. He always loved to entertain his friends, I seem to remember. I shall be inviting some of his old schoolmates – and of course, Lizzie and Gerald will be with us, won't they?'

Matt's heart swelled with supreme gratitude. He vowed that Mrs Nelligan would have the finest dinner his wife could plan and provide, and he decided, too, that it really was time the sound system was renewed; the screens which he used to partition the lounge from the dining room would do little to hinder the ability of bar patrons to hear any musical entertainment which might or might not be wafted over the loudspeakers. He was thankful that in Hackstown, as in most other Irish villages, the quickest method of spreading information was by word of mouth and a remark dropped quietly among the morning drinkers, that the world's most famous pop idol was going to be doing his thing privately for his friends, in the Castle Court dining room on a certain evening in the not too distant future, would ensure that by nightfall the news would have sped as far as Dublin, Donegal and Cork.

'Is he into antiques?' Marjorie asked hopefully. 'I've got a few rather charming early musical instruments and some old manuscripts he might like to have – and Aunt Ellen has promised me my great grandmother's spinet. He could have first refusal of that.'

'Pity he doesn't sound like he might be a sportsman,' said Geoffrey. 'The woods are alive with game these times – thanks to the fact that the Gun Club hasn't been blasting them out of the sky. And I think this season is going to be an excellent one for the fishing – I've given a great deal of attention to the trout stocks, so that we can be sure of having decent stretches for the enthusiasts among your expected tourists to fish in.' Agnes nodded. 'And did I tell you I have decided to have a little repair and supplies shop in operation?'

'How clever of you,' said Mrs Nelligan admiringly.

'Well, it struck me that most sportsmen have to leave their equipment to others to mend if anything goes wrong with it,' said Geoffrey. 'So I got together with Julian my brother, when he and his architect friend Simon were surveying the alterations for Marjorie. Julian is going to handle that side of the business for me – he's quite good with that sort of thing.'

A slight shadow swept over Geoffrey's countenance – Julian was not the sort of relation he would normally wish to discuss in public or even entertain down in Hackstown. He preferred to meet his brother no more than twice yearly in the city, where they could dine in a secluded eatery and where, hopefully, nobody knew either of them and Julian's friends, mostly bearing a clone-like similarity to Simon, would not mince in during the evening. Geoffrey rapidly changed the subject to a discussion about house property, with Billy Markey, and Mrs Nelligan appreciated his delicacy, although Julian's proclivities were not exactly unknown territory to her – after all, she reminded herself, the tendencies were so often present in the puberty wildernesses. Anyway, she quite liked Julian who had a marvellous way with fabrics, floral arrangements and, according to Marjorie, had an unerring eye when it came to recognising old glass.

'I suppose you'll be glad of your brother's company up at the House for the summer?' Billy said.

Geoffrey blanched. 'Good God, Julian won't be living with *us*!' he said hastily. 'Marjorie will have quite enough to do without having to look after my brother. He will be renting a place for himself.'

And as he thought of Julian's friends and the prospects of having to entertain them at Hackstown House, Geoffrey shuddered. This information cheered Mr Markey. By now Billy had all the available vacant properties well sewn up on his auctioneering books, and even if premises on offer for short lets were not as plentiful as one would have hoped, there were, he calculated, a few untapped sources which he had up to now not bothered about. Their owners were not prepared to part permanently with these premises, but they might well be highly interested in a rental agreement. Billy felt life was improving by the hour, even more so when later on in the day he got a chance to offer for rental three disused workmen's cottages which he straightaway put his daughter to redecorating and furnishing, on percentage, naturally, since she was in the middle of a most expensive correspondence course in interior decor. Billy felt she couldn't go overboard budget-wise on a few four-roomed cottages – which shows how wrong a loving male parent can be when he looses a daughter into any type of store, fashion or household. As he ruefully told Mrs Nelligan later, he should have been warned when he saw the doors being painted, puce, purple, electric blue and canary yellow, with window boxes to match. Still, they became quite a talking point in the village among the tourists. Billy dined out on it for months afterwards, when he rented one to a minor European Royal personage, who spent an entire summer season there with a live-in lover, whose main claim to fame appeared to be the size of the diamond stud in his left nostril.

'You do know, of course, that we'll have to invite the Minister for Leisure and Affiliated Arts to the Opening? He'll expect it,' reminded Charlie. 'And once he hears that Longbow is coming over, he'll miss a trip to America for Patrick's Day just to get on the same platform – it's one sure way of getting his face in the papers.'

'Himself and a few score more,' sniffed Billy. 'The big problem will be to control the numbers who will suddenly find they have a god-given right to be among the VIPs.'

'Well now,' smiled Mrs Nelligan, 'I've thought of that. So what we're going to do is to have the representatives from all the local bodies and organisations selected from among the young people and they will be voted for by our own people in Hackstown. Anyone else will be in the ordinary public audience of the assembly just as we will be – this is not going to be a day for personal ego-tripping. Anyway we'll have so many visitors, the best way to get the whole thing off the ground is to hold an open-air party and keep all the speeches to an absolute minimum – I've never found words to do more than fill in gaps at public functions. This time we will be filling in the gaps with happenings which will leave very little time for words!'

This idea pleased the village considerably. They had little desire to see their big day taken over by outsiders and publicity hunters, and Agnes had little difficulty in getting an enthusiastic working committee together to arrange this part of the proceedings, all of which left her free to take care of Longbow and any plans she intended to make for his visit.

Katie had also promised she would come to Ireland for the Opening and Mrs Nelligan expected Jonathan would manage to have himself included in the travel arrangements which Daniel was making for his television crew, even if Jonathan was not officially working with *Hogan's Hello*. At least she hoped so, because she was quite convinced that amongst the rural attractions of Hackstown, Katie would find it difficult to refuse any matrimonial proposal Jonathan might make, and that, Mrs Nelligan promised herself, was something Jonathan was going to put to her niece. Mrs Nelligan was not unaware of modern trends, but whatever was possibly going on in New York since her return to Ireland, she was determined that Katie was going to toe the social line like the majority of Irish females, and have a romantic white wedding with lace, flowers, tin cans and lucky horseshoes, and preferably right here in Hackstown's parish church. And she looked forward to meeting Daniel in her own surroundings, where she felt she would have some small advantage.

Her communication to Longbow was answered by an enthusiastic long transatlantic telephone call (listened to with mounting excitement at the local telephone exchange) from her ex-pupil, who accepted her invitation with flattering pleasure. Longbow wanted to go fishing, ride to hounds, sail a boat on Lough Bawn and make like a tourist – not only that, he wanted to stay for several days and try out the new beehive hut accommodations at the complex. He was, he said, bored to death with hotels, and it all sounded like a gas. And if she didn't mind, he'd probably bring along a little 'shiogue' of his own, and her name was Lisa. Mrs Nelligan didn't know whether to be vexed that Longbow was consorting with unmarried young women quite blatantly, or pleased that he still remembered even one of the Gaelic words she had so painfully instilled into his unwilling mind while he was at school. Under the circumstances, however, she was relieved that he wanted to investigate the delights of the new complex first-hand, though she doubted if his Lisa would be as adventurous. The beehive huts, while adequately furnished, were deliberately more functional than luxurious. Although, on second thoughts, for duvet lovers, the feather mattresses provided were an advance on sleeping comfort that would open up new delights.

A couple of weeks later a large truck rolled into Hackstown's village square, followed by a gleaming BMW, driven somewhat erratically. Out of the car descended a figure dressed in white trousers, pale pink suede jacket, white shoes and a black teeshirt, the front of which was emblazoned with a large pink and white cat, whose sequinned eyes looked in a rather lecherous fashion on a rural world which was not quite ready for the wearer of the finery. Slinging a white leather bag on one shoulder, the vision trotted into the lounge of the Castle Court Hotel and with a beaming smile, held out a delicately manicured hand to a stunned Matt Quinlan.

'Hiya! I'm looking for a Mrs Agnes Nelligan. I'm Alvin Randolph – I guess you know my Mom?'

Matt rushed around from behind the bar, shook Alvin's hand vigorously and sat him down at a table.'What will you have now?' he asked hospitably. 'A drop of whiskey or a pint?'

Alvin smiled. 'A glass of white wine, chilled if you please, and do you think you could manage to order me some lemon tea from your restaurant, and perhaps a little rye bread and some curd cheese?'

Matt stared at him in some puzzlement. He had to be mistaken, he told himself. This couldn't be related to the President of the United States. Alvin opened his shoulder bag and extracted a wad of pale pink facial tissues, mopping his forehead in the slightly fuggy atmosphere which was what the patrons of the Castle Court preferred in their drinking area.

Matt produced a glass of white wine with the speed of light, but he had to drop an ice cube into the glass in order to render it the required coolness for his important customer.

Alvin tutted slightly and removed the ice cube. But he nodded approvingly after he tasted the contents of the glass, which in fairness to Mr Quinlan was of top quality even when slightly diluted with an ice cube, Gerald having selected the wine stocks and vowed that average hotel plonk was outlawed at the Castle Court Hotel.

'And what brings you to Hackstown at this time?' Matt asked politely as he covertly studied Alvin and his sartorial delights. Maybe this was how modern youth dressed in Washington, he told himself, but he doubted it. In his heart he had instantly earmarked Alvin and something told him the most likely person with whom this young man would have total rapport was Geoffrey's brother Julian.

'I guess Mrs Nelligan has told you that I promised I would sculpt her a statue for the entrance of her new complex? Well, I have, and I decided I would come over myself and install it. I mean, who can you trust to display your work to best advantage other than yourself?'

Matt nodded again. Vaguely he recalled Agnes mentioning having backed into a diplomatic corner on the subject of Alvin's artistic creations. He was aware she had high hopes of getting the whole matter forgotten about in the subsequent activity, but now that Alvin had actually turned up complete with some excrescence or other, evidently big enough to need a truck to transport it, Matt could see problems ahead.

By now Alvin was half-way through his pot of tea and some of Mrs Quinlan's home-baked bread, which, even if it was not the requested rye variety, young Mr Randolph was tucking into with gusto. And the best the Castle Court could do in the way of curd cheese was a portion of a home-made goat cheese which Mrs Quinlan had managed to obtain from the nuns at the nearby convent, who were into wholefoods, free range eggs and goat milk.

'That was great!' said Alvin with satisfaction as he mopped up the last of the breadcrumbs from the plate. 'I went vegetarian a year ago; purity of diet gives purity of creativity, my tutor in Paris France used to say. But he always encouraged us to drink a little wine – for the soul's sake, he told us.'

Alvin failed to mention the fact that his erstwhile tutor was even now serving a term of incarceration for grossly indecent exposure while under the influence of the same wine he advised his students to sample sparingly. Which was what had brought Alvin back into the bosom of his family in Washington months before he was destined to return to the United States. Unfortunately for Alvin, he had been escorting the good professor back to his apartment after a night in one of the Left Bank establishments, when the marble nymph in the garden of a private house on the way there aroused the libido of his tutor and caused him to behave in what the judicial Maitre later described as an outrageous manner. Indeed, poor Alvin had to get his embassy to claim diplomatic immunity in order to prevent Alvin from sharing a cell with his tutor which would have been injustice of the gravest nature, since Alvin was so embarrassed by the female form that he was the only Art student at the Academy who had never attended a life class.

'What sort of statue might it be?' Matt enquired, watching with fascination as Alvin drew a white plastic-framed hand mirror from his bag and carefully removed any stray crumbs from the corners of his mouth. Matt observed a slight brownish-pink trace on the tissue and realised that Alvin was actually wearing a lip tint – subtly coloured it was true, but all the same definitely lipstick.

'It's real symbolic, that's what. Absolutely symbolic. I think it's just terrific! Quite the best thing I've ever done. Mom was just knocked out with it when I explained it to her.' Alvin rose. 'Well, I guess I'd better go find Mrs Nelligan. I know she'll sure want to see the statue just as soon as possible. I didn't manage to tell her I was coming over – I got a flight that could also ferry the sculpture and so I had to come when they made space available to me. I did try and telephone from the airport, but they didn't seem to be able to raise the exchange down here.'

Matt gave him directions to Mrs Nelligan's house, and Alvin climbed back again into his BMW which Matt could now see had diplomatic plates attached. He wobbled his way out of the village closely followed by the truck whose red-faced driver appeared to be holding a running conversation with himself as he tried to steer a course down the road which would avoid hitting Alvin in the rear, since the young man was obviously unsure of the steering power of the BMW and even less aware of the left-hand driving rule of the Irish roadway system.

Agnes was relaxing in her garden when Alvin and the truck halted at her gate. The young man was so pleased with himself and the surprise his arrival was obviously causing, that Mrs Nelligan hadn't the heart to show her opinion of Alvin's artistic talents. She fluttered and blinked her blue eyes at him and even the truck driver calmed down and thankfully accepted the large bottle of ale which she unearthed from the kitchen store cupboard where she had put it in readiness for the gardener when he came to cut the hedge. Taking her life in her hands, she bravely climbed into the passenger seat beside Alvin and directed him down the roadway to the complex, to which he was followed at a safe distance by the truck and driver. Fortunately for them, the construction crew were still on the site and between them and a hoist, they managed to disgorge the sculpture out of the truck.

With a flourish, Alvin removed the sacking covers from his work of art. Mrs Nelligan gave it a long look and then lost some of her rosy colouring.

The object was large, very large. In fact it stood a good six feet high and that was without the plinth which was standing beside it. Agnes was not quite sure just what it was meant to be or what it was made of. It appeared to consist of a large birdlike, cloaked figure, with a foot on a second recumbent birdlike figure (well, she believed they were birdlike figures since they both had nasal projectiles she calculated represented beaks). The figures were mounted on a mushroom-like base, edged with egg-shaped lumps, each lump being half-bisected by what afterwards turned out to be a bent tin can lid. The cloaked bird, which Mrs Nelligan had by now decided was definitely a vulture, had an odd-looking contraption stretching from one wing/hand: this was a slightly obscene-looking tubular item which she devoutly hoped would not be mistaken for a phallic symbol, and whose purpose in the entire she could not quite determine. The object ended in a gilded hoop resembling something half-way between a doughnut and a ring of black pudding, the circumference of which was studded with copper spikes of a most menacing appearance.

'I do hope you can see the symbolism of it,' Alvin said, trotting around his creation in some satisfaction. 'I entitled it "New Dawn" but Mom thought it would make it more interesting if we didn't title it at this time, but ran a contest among the tourists for the most suitable name and then I could do a smaller copy of it to give to the winner as the prize.' He smiled engagingly at Mrs Nelligan, looking so pleased with himself that she felt if he had been a puppy she would have found him a dog biscuit right away.

'It's ... individual,' she said delicately.

'Jasus!' said the truck driver after a prolonged circuit of the sculpture. 'If I saw that any Saturday night, I'd be down next mornin' to take the pledge for life!'

Alvin ignored him. 'It has a lot of hidden meaning, you know,' he said to Mrs Nelligan. 'The New Dawn is what you are trying to do here in Hickstown and the figures represent Success standing on Failure – but of course you probably saw that straight away. What might be more obscure are the series of Thought Drops which ring the foundation – the Thought Drops were the ideas needed to start the project going – and the tin pieces which are inset into the Thought Drops symbolise the basic tool of mankind, a simple blade to cut through all obstacles. And then that ring thing from the figure's hand, is the long road towards achievement leading up to that gilded crown of success with the golden rays coming from it. See – totally symbolic! Everyone was just knocked out with it back home.'

He stopped, slightly breathless, waiting for her comment. Mrs Nelligan pulled herself together.

'No one,' she said fervently, 'could have conceived it but you, my dear boy.'

Alvin was delighted. 'I knew it would get you where you live,' he said. 'Now, where are we going to site it?'

Two hours later, the construction team went on a sit-down strike. They refused, even for a bonus, to contemplate shifting the sculpture once more, Alvin having had it in every spare corner of the complex that had enough open ground to take the monstrous plinth it rested upon. By this time, it was standing at one end of a section earmarked to be used as a garden area to plant herbs and vegetables for any of the tourists interested in going the whole hog and eating like the ancient Celts, although Alvin was not then aware of the fact. Later "New Dawn" proved a godsend to keep the birds away from the peas and the beans, until events changed its ultimate fate.

Reluctantly, for he was loath to leave his work of art, Alvin drove himself back to the Castle Court, where he had the best Mrs Quinlan could do by way of a vegetarian dinner – a brown trout from the lake, a decent Irish baked potato and a blackberry tart, to gather the fruit for which she had no further to travel than her own back garden. Alvin was so fascinated at the idea of being able to go out and dig, pick or catch the food he would immediately consume, that it was with difficulty that Mrs Nelligan persuaded him to return to Washington and devote his attention to a new project she thought up to occupy him: the job of dreaming up a series of designs for monograms for the Tir na n-Og crockery, towels, and linen. By the time he actually got down to thinking about it, the complex was well into operation and Alvin had come out of his symbolic period and into what he termed his Peace Concept, in the pursuit of which he felt obliged to take an extended trip to San Salvador for on-the-spot inspiration.

However, on his return to America, Alvin did perform a useful function on behalf of Hackstown's Tir na n-Og. He did a first-class promotion job among the Back to Nature population on the fresh-food world to be found in Hackstown. All of which proved profitable later on for Geoffrey's fishing rights and provided an off-beat form of entertainment for a section of the tourists for whom a day's blackberry picking was an amusement voted as cute as leprechaun hunting.

Chapter Fourteen

It really was all coming together in a most satisfactory manner. Agnes couldn't have asked for more. Already television crews from the national station as well as from abroad had begun to set up their complicated operations for the official opening date. The street decorations were up for a three-mile radius around Hackstown and there were public toilets where no public toilets had ever been sited before, largely because, to Mrs Nelligan's infinite dismay, the First Lady had officially announced through her public relations unit, her embassy and all the American papers, that after all she would make a special trip for the opening of her Tir na n-Og. Although it was publicised as a private visit, unaccompanied by the President who was fully occupied with keeping his political head above water in the presidential primaries, the whole affair suddenly took on a more exciting aspect, and television producers saw the First Lady strolling through the ruins of her ancestral home, dining in the banquet room (now totally reconstructed by a newly formed American society calling itself the Friends of Illan) and even being persuaded to be photographed clasping an armful of Irish shamrock if they could manage to discover a clump big enough. But it did mean an invasion of security personnel into the village just when Hackstown could least afford the takeover which would inevitably ensue.

Lizzie had managed to complete her historical record (which was destined for the American best-seller lists in due course, offering the beautiful Liz a whole new lifestyle which she gleefully accepted, with the single proviso that Gerald should manage her affairs on a permanent basis). The book having been finished, Lizzie found herself at rather a loose end, which was not to her liking. She began to spend the odd morning serving behind the bar of the Castle Court lounge and even the Major developed a liking for her outrageous irreverence for the Establishment, Authority and the Government in general, even if he was sometimes reduced to a spluttering incoherence when she got started on the protection of wildlife.

For Lizzie was totally opposed to hunting, chasing, shooting, trapping or otherwise pursuing wild things of any shape or form. A prime protest marcher with the Society for the Protection of Wildlife, she was known to have spoiled several fox-hunts by the simple method of going out early enough and laying false trails over miles of countryside, as well as obtaining hundreds of signatures on protest petitions. She had made lists of friends and acquaintances with large tracts of good hunting territory in the provincial areas where the fox-hunts operated, persuading them to close their lands to the packs and riders, with considerable success. Lizzie was into Green Peace, seal protection, the care of badgers, otters, hares, and game birds, and the Major simply couldn't understand her attitude. But he admired her enthusiasm and he spent a good deal of time trying to come up with a way to turn it to his advantage. For Major Mulqueen was not finished with his fight to retain the shooting rights for Hackstown Gun Club. Tir na n-Og or not, there was still a fair bit of good bird country to make use of, and before they got into expansion plans, the Major was determined to wage another battle or two. True, his immediate troops were pretty thin on the ground, being now depleted to the few tweedy ladies, a few non-local, weekend shooting enthusiasts who drove down from the city a few times during the season, and the local beater who, after all, had a vested interest in keeping his job of flushing out the pheasant continuing to function. The rest of the Gun Club members had blatantly sold out to what the Major could only believe was the worst form of Capitalism, the potentially successful kind. He had written endless letters, to the Irish President, the First Lady herself, to the Archbishop, to the Commissioner of Police, the Head of the Ancient Order of Hibernians, the Knights of Columbanus, the Grand Masonic Lodge, the Daughters of Israel, and even the Council of Europe and the EEC. All he got back was a lengthy and incomprehensible form from Brussels, giving him details of a subsidy which might be his to claim if he decided to re-export hides, feathers, treated dried skins or carcases or any processed products therefrom, none of which was of any real assitance to him.

Then, a week before Opening Day, Major Mulqueen got what he believed was an absolutely inspired idea. It was not exactly ethical, but, as he told himself, desperate situations took desperate measures to resolve. He laid his plans most carefully, and told no one of what he had in mind. The old strategy of surprise, he reminded himself, was still the most valuable asset in any campaign.

He waited until Lizzie and her friends were enjoying their evening drinks in the courtyard of the hotel, which they had begun to patronise on a nightly basis, now that the warmer evenings had arrived, and Matt had put out the patio tables and the Martini umbrellas.

Ostensibly buried in his copy of *The Field and Gun* the Major listened to their general conversation, part of which appeared to be a discussion on the most effective method of mounting a protest against fashion-trade use of certain rare animal skins for garments for the couture business – Lizzie having already announced her refusal to model a fur collection destined for the coming autumn. One of the more aggressive of the group was full of plans to break into some of the leading fur stores and remove the stock, while the earnest Emily favoured writing to leading personalities of the fashion world asking for their support against the wearing of real fur under any circumstances. It was time, the Major felt, to advance his own suggestion.

'One of the greatest offenders I know is the lady who is coming to Ireland next week to visit Hackstown,' he remarked to no one in particular, as he snapped open a small suitcase he had on a chair beside him.

'Really?' said Lizzie, without too much interest – the Major was not one of her more favourite acquaintances.

'Yes. Look at all these photographs and the write-ups from various magazines and newspapers,' said the Major, handing over a sheaf of clippings to the group who by now were listening with a sudden renewal of attention.

'The President of America's wife, there she is, big and bold, and almost every time she's been photographed, she's been covered in the skin of some animal or other – ocelot, leopard, mink, and I hear she was given a baby-seal jacket from some grateful North American delegation or other. If you wanted to make your point, the one to protest about would be Madam herself,' said Major Mulqueen firmly.

Lizzie looked at him. 'How come you're so concerned, Major?' she queried. 'You hunt foxes and shoot birds, don't you?'

'My dear young woman,' replied Major Mulqueen with a pained expression. 'Foxes are vermin and birds are food. I don't hold with slaughtering wild or rare animals simply to put their pelts on the backs of women who wouldn't even know how to shiver. Why, my own wife doesn't own a fur coat – I have Principles!' He quite neglected to tell them that it was because he was much too mean to replace it, that Mrs Mulqueen had to trot out her moth-eaten sheepskin coat year after year when her greatest dream was to own the best simulation mink that money could buy – Mrs Mulqueen being an active member of the Beauty Without Cruelty brigade.

They went through the cuttings he had spent a good week getting together from all the back issues of the magazines being used by the papier mâché workers, who had obliged him with the clippings for a consideration.

'You know, he's right,' Emily's friend Jason said. 'That woman has eight fur coats by my count, and they all look like the real thing.'

'So, let's stage a massive protest here, then,' said Alastar. 'With the crowds coming to the opening of the complex, we'll get the maximum effect and we'll do a proper job – no mickey-mouse banners or stickers, but massive banners and streamers and a march. We might even manage to dress a float with some sort of protest tableau.' They gathered around excitedly at one of the tables near the Major, ignoring him as someone dragged out a notebook and they got a meeting going on the spot.

The Major smiled quietly. After a while, he signalled Matt to bring fresh drinks out. The group, never loath to accept a free beer when it was offered, thanked him politely, and then the Major produced his suggestions.

'Why don't you stage a sit-down protest at the complex and do a twenty-four-hour vigil with torchlight and have music? If you wait until the day of the opening, the roadway could be blocked off and you would have to protest on the perimeter of the grounds which would not be nearly so effective. I am sure more of your friends would want to join you in such a valuable exercise, against what a great many people believe is an unnecessary practice.'

Lizzie's friends were delighted with the idea. A torchlight sit-in with the chance of a twenty-four-hour jazz session thrown in was an item that found instant favour. It was far less troublesome to arrange than a decorated float, and the banners were standard property with most self-respecting student groups. They scattered to contact friends, fellow protestors, musicians, and anyone who would be in sufficient funds to bring along the nourishment for mind and body to last out the forty-eight hours. It was planned to occupy the laneway to the complex. The Major actually promised delivery of two crates of lager and volunteered to contact his fellow members in the city, who might also be prepared to deliver additional assistance of a liquid nature to a drop-off in Dublin.

Lizzie somewhat reluctantly decided that it would be wiser if she neglected to tell Gerald of the protest sit-in arrangements. She felt a little guilty about mounting a protest at all in Hackstown since it might well affect the plan the village had given so much effort to putting into operation. And of course, apart from Mrs Nelligan, for whom Lizzie had a very soft spot, there was Gerald's disco and Matt's big night at the hotel to consider. But there was also the fate of all those poor little animals to bear in mind, she consoled herself. They would not fail to benefit from a much publicised protest such as the one they were now putting together, and she felt sure that when she explained to them, the people of Hackstown would surely accept that they were really only temporarily being somewhat discommoded. Or so she hoped.

The Major also was keeping quiet about his newest band of reinforcements. This was one time, he swore, that Mrs Agnes Nelligan would not be able to shove her busybody nose into his plans. Major Mulqueen grew quite unchristian whenever he thought about Mrs Nelligan. She was having too much success with her plans altogether, he told himself crossly. Nothing, but nothing, had gone wrong for her and her damned committees and co-operatives. It was most galling to observe Geoffrey in his new shop, working all the hours God sent, with fishing and shooting enthusiasts practically queuing up to have their rods and guns put into top working order by that poofter of a brother of Geoffrey's, who, he hated to admit, was fast building up a solid reputation for excellent workmanship, particularly when it came to fly tying. And Geoffrey's deer herd could be seen roaming all over the blasted woods so that a body couldn't even spring a rabbit in case the dog came up against a hind and attacked it. Futhermore, the Marjorie woman was cleaning up in her antique shop and his own wife was actually helping in the place every day – and not only that, but finding a flair for upholstery she never realised she had. He hardly ever saw her for meals any more, and he had no one to complain at during luncheon, which quite took the edge off his day. In fact, had he thought of it, the Major would have come to the conclusion that the only one not gainfully employed for, in, on behalf of, or because of, the Hackstown Tir na n-Og, was himself. And all this was before the damned place even opened! What it would be like *then* he shuddered to think. The village would be in a state of perpetual motion and would certainly go down in history as the smallest area with the largest proportion of millionaires outside of Texas, if you took his drift.

He spent long hours in the garden shed, designing and making up a special placard for the sit-in – naturally he was going to be a part of the protest, even if the group were as yet unaware of the fact. He offered facilities to Lizzie's friend Emily, to come and make up the banners on his premises –

that way he was able to keep an expert eye, as he called it, on what the content matter of the slogans was going to be. Emily was rather intimidated by Major Mulqueen; he was very like her mother in attitude, and she was easily pressurised into agreement that the placards should be as brief as possible – in fact the Major volunteered to write them himself.

The finished slogans were brief – very brief and very basic. They carried words like 'Hands Off' and 'Stop Now', and he brushed aside Emily's plaintive requests for something a little more militant like 'Save Our Animal Friends' or 'Would You Kill the American Eagle for its Feathers?' The Major didn't like such sentiments at all; they were likely to lead to a breach of the peace, he told her loudly, and this was to be a peaceful protest or the police would move them on before the First Lady turned up at all. Emily subsided.

The day before the official opening, Hackstown was filled to overflowing. Most of the populace was composed of outsiders, the locals being up to their armpits in preparations for the first day of Hackstown's expected High Life. TV crews darted like misshapen monkeys in and out of laneways and alleyways, the cameras ever whirring and, it would seem, permanently attached to the shoulders of the frenetic young men carrying them about. Tourists were in dire danger of causing grass fires, there was so much flash-bulb popping and lenses catching the rays of the summer sun. In the village square the game of the day was the continuous upturning of the rows of the chairs, borrowed from the local school, which had been laid out in readiness for the official speech-making on the following day. Hackstown's policeman, Johnnie Fennessey, had long given up the unequal struggle with the village juveniles who, on the long summer holidays from lessons, were, at this stage of the season, avid for some variety to come into their lives, and upturning the chairs was a diversion not to be ignored.

The Castle Court Hotel was jumping. Gerald and Matt were serving drinks, sandwiches and lunches at a gallop and Lizzie was managing to be in four different places at once, much to the delight of the drinkers out on the patio, for whom her arrival at regular intervals with trays of nourishment was a classic titillation, Lizzie being clad for comfort in a pale lemon-yellow cheesecloth dress which against the sunlight was semi-transparent and showed her quite splendid limbs to perfection.

Daniel, his crew and Jonathan had already arrived and were ensconced in the Castle Court, while Katie was settled in at Mrs Nelligan's cottage and looking as if she would never leave it again. Which was very understandable, for Mrs Nelligan's home was the sort of domicile which, if seen in a guide book, would immediately make the viewer discontented with whatever house he owned. It had oak beams, an inglenook with a floor level fire and a bellows wheel set into the wall. It had copper and brass ware, ruby glassware, hooked rugs, a verandah running the entire length of one side which was set with chairs that wrapped themselves around a tired body and caressed it to new life.

The garden had two levels reached by old stone steps. It had a small reeded rock-pool with a tiny natural waterfall, and it boasted of old-fashioned flowers like hollyhocks, petunias, lavender and rosemary and a little willow tree. It was called Heron's Rest simply because there was actually a heron who came every year to nest by the river which fed the garden pond. Katie instantly adored it. She sat contentedly for hours on the verandah and every day at four o'clock, Jonathan's tall figure would saunter in the gate, just in time for the tea and tiny shortbread biscuits which Mrs Nelligan served to sustain them until dinner time. Two days after he had arrived, Daniel had adopted the routine and had surprised himself by developing quite a taste for the China tea Agnes produced, even if his hands found it slightly traumatic trying to handle with a degree of safety the delicate china cups in which she delivered the pale amber brew.

The four of them sat, watching the last of the sun dappling the edges of the lily pond, contentedly silent in the warmth of the afternoon.

'This is the life, you know,' said Katie, brushing back her dark auburn hair which she was wearing loose about her shoulders for greater coolness. 'I don't know how I shall bear it when I have to go back to New York. This really is the darlingest little house I have ever seen, Aunt Agnes. I don't blame you for wanting to spend as much time as you possibly can in it.'

'I am so glad you like it my dear, because some day you will most certainly own it. Originally, this house belonged to my great great grandparents – our family has had its roots in Hackstown for nearly two hundred years, you know. I would like to think you will carry on the tradition, since I have no children of my own to hand it on to.'

Katie sparkled with delight and Jonathan looked at her with a sudden despair. If his beautiful Katie came back to Ireland how would he ever manage to make her marry him? He wasn't having much luck so far in selling Katie the idea that her entire future happiness lay in keeping house, home and at least three new little Hogans, well fed, watered and loved. And while equality was the in-thing with modern women, he was slightly old-fashioned when it came to being happy that the woman he loved to distraction was probably making twice the income he was, even if he could fairly claim that what the taxman left him was quite respectable.

And Daniel, too, felt a small cold wind of depression go over him. Of course Agnes wanted to stay in Hackstown, and Heron's Rest, as any sane person would. What had New York to offer which would prove superior to herons in one's garden, or trout rivers that nuzzled their way over granite rocks collapsing in little pools full of hysterical minnows? What inducements had New York's theatreland got when an hour's driving on pleasantly quiet roadways would bring a drama-loving native into the heart of the Irish metropolis where most good shows turned up eventually anyhow? Daniel had long come to the conclusion that there was a life after First Nights. A flicker of something he could not define seemed to extinguish itself in his mind and he felt unaccountably tired.

Katie eyed Hogan senior, and hid a small grin as she saw his expression change from its customary businesslike look to something rather small-boyish and lost. So *that* was how the land lay, she told herself. It would take a firm-minded, sensible girl like herself to manipulate those two into becoming aware of each other and she would have to give her attention to the matter before they all returned to America and Agnes did something stupid like becoming a Managing Director of some international organisation or other. And Mrs Nelligan caught a glimpse of Jonathan's frown and spotted the droop of his shoulders as he suddenly got up from his relaxer chair and made much of gathering the crockery on to its tray before carting it back into the kitchen. The time was about ripe for Katie to acquire some sense, she reminded herself, before she let that delightful young man slip through her fingers and into the arms of some young flittery-gibbet back in New York, or worse still, a blow-in at the hotel perhaps.

'Would your film crew enjoy a midnight banquet in the old castle ruins?' she asked Daniel suddenly. 'You know that the main banquet hall has been restored, so that they would have somewhere to eat in comfort, and of course the river is shallow enough for bathing in, and it is such an attractive area, particularly when the moon is up.' She smiled deprecatingly. 'I know, of course, that your people are used to more sophisticated entertainment, but for its novelty value perhaps, they might care to sample a medieval Irish evening's music and song, and as you know, we have dancers, pipers and an excellent flute player. Your personnel might enjoy one of the more unusual entertainments Hackstown will be offering its visitors.'

'Great!' said Daniel enthusiastically. 'We'll bring the booze, and you bring the food and entertainment. Tomorrow we'll all be working flat out for the opening of Tir na n-Og, so let's have a good time tonight.'

They were not the only folk to be abroad. By now, all two hundred of Lizzie's friends and associates had slowly found their various ways to Hackstown and were ensconced at the communal camping ground where they were gainfully employed in getting hyped up for the march and sit-in. They presented a colourful sight and were so well conducted that Lizzie was proud of them. Carefully she explained the purpose of their protest, the need for order and peace, and the importance of the whole project to the village. (In fact, she was so dedicated to Hackstown's project that a fair number of the crowd were fired with a desire to join the commercial rat race in Hackstown, and remained on to go into business for themselves later.) The music was subdued and, for the most part, genteel. Then, accompanied by loud hiccupping sounds from the faulty exhaust on his ancient and temperamental station wagon, the Major arrived with Emily cowering in the front seat as far away from him as she could squeeze, and the back of the wagon was filled with the placards and banners over which they had both worked throughout the week.

He rallied the group like an army squad into a disorderly procession. When he had them two by two, he jerked a thumb at Emily to hand out the placards. The marchers on whom she bestowed the painted wooden sheets with their broom handles looked at them in some surprise. The Major ran from section to section, rearranging the placard holders with the admonition that under no circumstances were they to move from the places he had given them. He left a bank of six couples between each placard carrier and he was careful to place Lizzie at the head of the marchers and gave her the portable loudspeaker to take care of, which was why she didn't get an over-view of the entire procession when it began to move in the direction of the leisure complex entrance gates, with the Major bearing up in the rear.

Major Mulqueen had painted his slogans in luminous paint and in the summer darkness, the words stood out defiantly. The protest marchers filled the laneway and on the Major's advice, they planted their placards firmly in the soft grassy shoulder of the laneway. And by the time that Mr Nelligan and her guests made their way to the ruins of Illan castle, not only was the laneway blocked off well and truly by two hundred guitar-playing, chanting, singing, happily relaxed protestors, but thanks to Major Mulqueen's arrangements, a message in luminous paint was being spelled out for all to see. Collectively, the placards advocated 'STOP NOW. IT'S UNSPORTING. HANDS OFF. HACKSTOWN GUN CLUB', the last placard being tightly held by the Major, determined that no one would wrest it from him in the event of any objection arising.

Mrs Nelligan ran her eye over the total message and her lips tightened as she took in the situation. She spotted Lizzie happily singing at the head of the crowd, quite obviously, in company with the rest of her companions, unaware of the perfidy of the Major and his manipulation of her friends.

'Lizzie, my dear,' she called, and Lizzie came to her side, blushing slightly with embarrassment.

'You are an advocate of blood sports, suddenly?' queried Mrs Nelligan while Lizzie looked at her in complete puzzlement. Agnes gestured to the line of placards and Lizzie, once she picked out the slogan, grew very angry indeed.

'He told us that the President's wife was into wearing real furs, and that she owns at least eight fur coats and wraps, so we felt it would be the time to point out to her that it was a highly uncivilised attitude to take when animals were being slaughtered to provide her with her overcoats. That's why we decided to march – we didn't want to harm Hackstown, you understand – but it was a marvellous opportunity to make a stand for animal welfare.'

Mrs Nelligan nodded sympathetically. 'Have you got the pictures he showed you?' she asked, and within minutes, Jason had brought the package of magazine cuttings to them. Mrs Nelligan studied them carefully and then handed them over to Katie.

'Well now, these are at least four years old, I can tell you,' said Katie after a careful glance through the batch. 'That neckline was first featured back in 1980 and I recall she bought that evening gown when the President first ran for office – as a matter of fact, I had to stock several copies of it for my customers. And I can tell you that after he got into office, she gave up wearing real furs completely and has since become President of the American Fur and Feather Society, a patron of the North American Wildlife Group, and with regard to that seal jacket Major Mulqueen made so much about, she donated it to raise funds for the Society for the Protection of Arctic Animals. So on the face of it, your protest is somewhat unnecessary, though it is obvious that the Major can use it very well for his own ends, if you allow it to continue.'

Lizzie nodded. She was furious. It took no length for her to send her scouts through the crowd and as if by magic every placard came down. The protestors decided a jazz session was in order. Within minutes, Major Mulqueen found it impossible to get sense from anyone, even if he had been able to make himself heard above the music. Some time later, someone heard a newscast on one of the transistors, that a group of students was staging a massive protest against a proposal to build a nuclear power station along the eastern coast of the country. Within an hour, they had, to a man, departed en masse to give the newest project their enthusiastic support and assistance, leaving a mere half-dozen of their number to clear up the mess of litter and discarded placards.

Peace once more descended on the laneway and the now deserted Tir na n-Og, whose shiny newly painted huts, restaurants, leisure areas and entertainment annexes awaited the summer holiday-makers. But the midnight banquet was in full swing and in between the medieval measures and roundelays, Mrs Nelligan watched her niece and the handsome Jonathan being crowned as the king and queen of the castle and hosts of the banquet. But even in all the moonlight and with the undoubted romance which surrounded them, she was disappointed in the results. Katie did not come to her, all starry-eyed, and announce a pending marriage. In fact she was much more excited over an idea she had had to design a new range of clothes inspired by the medieval times they had just been commemorating. And they were two of a pair. Jonathan was full of plans to do a documentary about the First Lady's ancestors, using the castle as his background. Mrs Nelligan's romantic heart despaired of them. But for the moment, her plans had to go on hold until Opening Day was over.

Chapter Fifteen

Opening Day dawned with the sort of soft warm wind and brilliant morning sunshine that promised hours of perfect weather. No one was surprised; the weather would not have dared to disappoint Mrs Nelligan.

Longbow had turned up late in the night and was now lying flat on his back in Mrs Nelligan's guest bedroom, making unlovely snoring sounds, undisturbed by traffic, telephones, or agents yabbering about recordings and contracts. At a morally safe distance down the road in Mrs Mulqueen's spare room, a somewhat surprised Lisa, Longbow's little 'shiogue', was installed, and in the process of being completely taken over by Mrs Mulqueen's white cat. Longbow and Lisa had been in a distinct state of coolness on the way down to Hackstown because his lady-love would not believe Longbow when he assured her that his Irish pet name for her really meant to flatter her. It took Mrs Nelligan's gentle explanation that the Gaelic word for a fairy was totally a feminine term and had absolutely no sexual associations in the Irish language. Once she discovered she was about to be farmed out to alternative sleeping arrangements, however, Lisa was convinced that not only the language but the entire country must be asexual as well, from which one can deduce that the lovely Lisa's talents were not intellectual, cultural or even social. Her interests were on no higher a plane either and two days of Longbow tasting the country pleasures of Hackstown and Tir na n-Og bored his lady to such a degree that she hightailed it out of the village to Monaco, where a past benefactor and his yacht were fortuitously tied up and anxious for the company of a well-stacked bird who knew better where she was when someone called her a living doll than when she was described as an Irish fairy, no matter how well meant.

She would have been highly unsuitable for Longbow, Mrs Nelligan observed to herself later, when in some satisfaction she noted the success of her arrangements to separate them as painlessly as possible. Mrs Nelligan believed in manipulation without confrontation wherever possible.

Thanks to her arrangements with his fan clubs and the local youth associations, Longbow was left in almost total peace and privacy without being hounded at every turn, so much so that he spent his second morning scouring the countryside with Billy Markey, looking at houses so that he could buy one before he went back to the States. It was, he remarked with relief, the first time he had got off to sleep without the help of a pill for the past couple of years, and he wanted more of it. If he could relax and be his own man in Hackstown, without young women leaping from every corner rending his jacket off, then the obvious thing to do was to find a house in the rural peace of the village. And amazingly, in Billy's opinion, the property Longbow fell for was one Billy was having considerable trouble trying to move. In fact it had been on his books for nearly two years. It was a long, low, farmhouse of indefinite age, set up a laneway so overgrown that sometimes even the locals forgot the house was actually there at all. But it had a little wood of copper beeches, a tiny lake that just missed being a pond, and the remains of a cobbled patio where Longbow determined he would sit through the summer days and get inspiration for more chart-topping musical masterpieces. The fact that the house had no electricity, got its water supply from a well in the back yard, and needed glass in most of its windows, did nothing to deter his enthusiasm for the place, and Billy, it must be said, urged him to look around at several other houses which at least could boast of power at the pull of a switch and a decent back door, which he also had on his list of desirable properties. Longbow knew his own mind. In an hour, he handed over the cheque and told Billy to get a team of workmen on to the place immediately as he expected to move into it within a month when he would return and take his summer break there instead of keeping to his original plan to take his entire entourage to Bermuda. All of which he subsequently did.

From early morning, the crowds were congregating in Hackstown. By eleven o'clock, there wasn't a parking spot for miles, a vacant picnic area or a spot one could set down a folding canvas chair. All the good vantage places were long gone and the rows of chairs around the official dais were occupied very early on by the determined-looking locals whose children were representing the societies and organisations, and the hangers on of the various political parties had to make do with the perimeter of the square, where they were most unlikely to get photographed.

At two o'clock precisely, the cavalcade with the First Lady securely positioned amongst a quartet of motor-cycle outriders and four cars of American security mohair suits, whirled into the village. They were met with ceremony by the local dignitaries and as many political representatives as could not be left out of the day's activities. The First Lady wore a fetching bright green suit and cream leather accessories. Between the green suit and the red hair, you could mistake her for a set of traffic lights, one slightly jaundiced lady journalist commented rather sourly in her column next day, the Irish being anything but flattered when their national colour turns up being used for what they regard as purely political flattery. Mrs Nelligan knew that the simpler vote appeal policies of the Americans were not capable of understanding the deviousness of Gaelic methodology, and she was ready to forgive the First Lady most things just as long as she stuck around long enough to confirm that Hackstown was to hold the title deeds to the 150 acres in perpetuity to do with as it wished. One had, she knew, particularly in the light of the Irish political climate, to be able to look ahead and adjust plans accordingly, and the freedom to manoeuvre was vital for the members of Hackstown Tir na n-Og committee, if the complex was going to grow and perhaps diversify in the future.

The hand-shaking and the speech-making completed, the First Lady officially handed over the Deed of Perpetuity which was even larger and more ornately printed and decorated than the one she had bestowed on Mrs Nelligan in Washington. Matt Quinlan promptly installed it in a glass case which had already been prepared, on the wall of the Castle Court Hotel, where with due gravity a golden lock and key secured it from the light-fingered behind bullet-proof glass.

Then the party took itself out to Tir na n-Og to have a private look around. Alvin, by now safely ensconced down in San Salvador, had urged his mother to take photographs for him of his sculpture. She came, armed with numerous cameras to do his bidding as loving mothers usually do, but somehow, even the devotion of a mother has to know when defeat stares her in the face. Alvin's sculpture was so large and ungainly that no angle seemed to do anything for it, added to which, by now, it was covered with bird droppings, and a couple of smart blackbirds had taken over the crown of success between the spokes of which they had managed to build a sizeable nest, from whose confines they cursed the assembly in a highly raucous fashion.

The First Lady stared uncertainly at the sculpture, her maternal eye at last having to face the very obvious.

'My Gaad!' she exclaimed. 'I never realised that thing would seem so big. I never did get a look at it on its plinth. It seems as high as the Statue of Liberty. It's – well – sorta – overpowering, isn't it?' She walked around it again.

Everyone nodded, none of them trusting themselves to find the most judicious remark to make. The First Lady removed her high heel from an unexpected rabbit hole.

'Not that I don't think it has – well – Perspective – you understand. Alvin explained it all to me and of course, he has an inner vision special to artists. I don't really come to grips with it myself ... But it's just that I somehow didn't think it all looked so ... so ... overpowering now that it's installed.' She smiled at Mrs Nelligan almost hopefully. 'Still, I daresay the place is big enough to take it and Alvin was so pleased you were impressed with his talent. That boy has a humility that's quite overwhelming, don't you think?'

Fortunately, Mrs Nelligan could see that her question was more or less rhetorical, which saved Agnes the necessity of bending the truth – a habit she never encouraged her pupils to indulge in and therefore one which came uneasily to her in the rare times her supreme tact caused her to resort to it.

Even though the residential section of Hackstown's Tir na n-Og was not yet in operation, the entertainment and leisure sections were in the main ready for testing out. On the lake, Mr Okami's swan boats were bobbing, white paintwork gleaming, the golden crowns on the swans' heads glittering with glass jewel insects among the gilt enamelling, the simulated precious stones as impressive as the real thing. A quartet of chariots with unlikely looking Gaelic scrollwork painted all over them were dashing up and down, drawn by a pair of white and a pair of black horses decked out in a harness and cloth which most foreign visitors later believed was an Irish equestrian kilt, but which to tell the truth, was a mind bending traumatical experience to the Connemara ponies, who spent the summer trying to paw their way out of it. On one of the flat stretches of the complex near the upper end of the lake, the Battle of the Boyne was fought twice daily, and it was quite an impressive sight to see a convoy of boats, designed after the Norse vessels which had once sailed up the River Liffey, doing their best to row across Lough Bawn, while keeping the sails up at the same time.

They even led the First Lady to a little mound, one of the marks on the Treasure trail, where, with great ceremony, she was permitted to discover the first of the Swords of Finn McCool, Ireland's historic warrior, an impressive object on which Mr Okami had spent a fair share of cash, believing that so important an artefact could not be produced on mickey-mouse lines if he were to ensure the continuation of this very lucrative sideline which tourists were ecstatic to 'dig up' and eager to smuggle home in their airline grips.

In all, the First Lady had a highly entertaining day and it was with some regret when the banquet at her ancestral hall was still in full swing, that she took her leave of Mrs Nelligan and the village.

'I hate to go, but my husband really needs me to be with him – else they'll let him make a fool of himself at some venue or other,' she confided to Agnes before she finally whirled away in the embassy limousine to the airport. She opened her handbag and took out a set of shiny new keys and handed them to Mrs Nelligan.

'When the winner of the TV competition is drawn on *Hogan's Hello* I want you to give them the use of the Presidential beehive hut you so kindly presented to us,' she said quickly. 'I think that whoever wins might get a buzz out of staying in it, and one satisfied customer can send you a dozen new clients. You can return them to me when you come back to America which I hope will be real soon, now you hear?'

She smiled, hugged Mrs Nelligan and was gone before Agnes could thank her. And her opinion turned out to be spot on. When, in an unprecedented high-speed appearance on Daniel's show, Longbow drew the winner of the free trip to Hackstown, the winner turned out to be an Italian wine importer with six children and a family of relatives as myriad as a field of daisies. They later made impressive block bookings and could be said to have established the first Italian ghetto in rural Ireland.

It was with considerable relief that the residents of Hackstown saw the departure of officialdom and the guardians of public safety from the village by nightfall. So much watchfulness was putting quite a damper on the various rural pastimes beloved by the natives.

Hackstown's only policeman Johnnie Fennessey had better things to do than patrol the highways and byways, the twelve public houses and the genteel places of amusement, so that little matters like after-hours drinking, games of Pitch and Toss, poker schools and the like, flourished in the same orderly fashion as they had always done, with mutual respect for the parameters of good taste and tolerance. But for the few days the outsiders had been in the village, they harassed the natives considerably, and anyone out and about after dark was subjected to a stop and question routine which Hackstown resented. Johnnie himself was exhausted after a spell of duty which would have flattened a younger and fitter man. Once he saw the last black car on its way back to the city, he thankfully removed his uniform, replaced his boots with a pair of comfortable slippers and flopped down into his armchair before the television, determined that nothing short of an armed invasion would get him out again.

It was an important night for the Castle Court Hotel. For one thing, Longbow was being entertained to dinner as arranged, while Gerald and Lizzie were opening the Dungeon Disco at midnight. But at eleven o'clock, Longbow had a most important date to keep out at the Tir na n-Og grounds: he was going to switch on the illuminations and light the first firework in what was going to be the definitive of all firework displays. His cavalcade was reminiscent of the Pied Piper: almost everyone followed him out to the complex, complete with torches, musical instruments, flags, whistles and the odd bottle of wine.

The complex was in total darkness when the procession reached the gates. The committee was lined up on either side of the gates with Mrs Nelligan in the middle, carrying a pair of golden scissors. There was a two-inch-wide golden satin ribbon tying the ornate gateway which Markey had found abandoned at an old country estate five miles up the road, and salvaged for the entrance to the complex. Longbow, with a fine sense of the theatrical, brandished the golden scissors aloft, snipped the ribbons, and then, as the gates swung open, he reached to the systems box which was housed inside the gates, pulled the lever and lit up Hackstown's Tir na n-Og to a glittering beginning. There were winking lights, blinking lights, running lights, static lights, spotlights, hidden illuminations – in fact the electrical contractor had created a magical effect. There were coloured lights festooned around the little slipway at the lake where the swan boats were tied up, and over the gateway, a fairy with a wand of coloured bulbs was permanently dancing back and forth across the wrought-ironwork. Then Longbow lit the first firework, and as it took off into the night sky it could be seen that it resembled a leprechaun in sparkling green irridescence. The display lasted almost half an hour, after which, with no little triumph, the entire procession removed itself back to the courtyard of the Castle Court Hotel to continue the celebrations.

A fair proportion of the same crowd was composed of Lizzie's friends back in force from their nuclear protest march and most willing to support her newest venture. They were happily doing their own thing in the courtyard with competent musical backing of instruments as diverse as a tin whistle, guitar, balalaika and button accordion, depending on whether the owner was into traditional, folk, or jazz music. Emily – who had, she felt, vindicated her previous mishap of trusting the Major when she pointedly walked up to him in the Square, handed him back his bundle of banners which she had removed from their support stakes and told him of an action which might provide him with an alternative use for his placards – now quietly sipped a glass of wine at a corner table in the courtyard.

Now Emily had one small talent, largely unpublished: she sang quite good flamenco, having spent several summers working in Spain's Andalusia. There was something about the music that grabbed her and she happily experimented in the privacy of her bed-sitter back in the city, until she too could execute a quite competent flamenco in a voice that was, when one regarded Emily's personal timidity, surprisingly powerful and confident. Still listening to her companions playing some Irish folk music, Emily suddenly had an irresistible urge to make her own music. She began to experiment with mating a Spanish flamenco treatment to one of Ireland's oldest folk tunes, and the result was electrifying.

There was an instant hush, as Emily, eyes closed, head thrown back, worked her way through 'Roisin Dubh' in a way that it had never been heard before, quite unconscious that she was actually giving a performance. Inside in the dining room, Longbow suddenly put down his knife and fork as he heard the unorthodox sounds coming from the courtyard. Mrs. Nelligan was puzzled for a moment too, until she recognised the basic line of the music.

'Good heavens! Someone is turning "My Dark Rosaleen"

into a flamenco song,' she said in surprise. Longbow nodded, mesmerised.

'It's fantastic,' he breathed. 'Who on earth is doing it? She's terrific!'

He leaped up and shot out of the dining room into the courtyard in time to catch Emily working her song to an exhilarating finish, in good honest Spanish fashion. She stood, clad in a bunchy white cotton top and skinny pink cotton trousers, her fair hair tied back with a pink ribbon, and Longbow thought she was the nicest thing he had ever seen or heard. He pushed his way through the crowd, who, recognising him began to murmur excitedly and several of them tried to hang on to his arms. Longbow brushed them aside and made his way with the speed of light to Emily's side. He was terrified she would disappear before he reached her. Emily finished her song, opened her eyes and realised where she was, and blushed prettily. She sat down again in some confusion. Longbow stood over her taking both her hands in his. 'Where did you learn to do that with Irish music and what's your name?' he asked.

'Spain, and it's Emily,' she told him, gulping slightly when she realised who was asking.

'Come into the hotel with me and we'll talk,' said Longbow. 'Come and have dinner with us – please.'

By now he was surrounded by fans, and as the whirl of bodies clustered around him, he was swept away from the table, and physically lifted up on to a stone step which was once used as a mounting block for the ladies who patronised the local hunt. And because he was still holding on to Emily's hands, she, perforce, had to go along with him, pushed by the enthusiastic crowd, until they were both lifted on to the step and planked firmly in full view of the courtyard audience.

'Gee, it's our Emily!' said Lizzie as she caught sight of the couple in the crush of the crowd. Longbow grabbed hold of a proffered guitar from the crowd and without more ado, struck up what he profoundly hoped was a fair copy of the opening bars of a flamenco tune, nodded encouragingly to Emily and then when Emily converted to an old Irish ballad tune, both of them began to vocalise. Emily led, Longbow followed and his fans, always eager to approve, clapped in reasonably appropriate places. For nearly an hour, they both sang until Longbow suddenly realised he had left his hostess somewhat precipitately, and called a halt. Then he put a careful arm around a bemused Emily, ushered her into the hotel dining room where neither of them really saw anyone else, or even tasted the remainder of the excellent meal cooked by Mrs Quinlan, so engrossed in each other did they become.

Mrs Nelligan was delighted. Emily, she felt, needed a caring young man like Longbow to protect her from opportunistic bullies such as her mother and the Major, while she would be absolutely ideal to make Longbow happy. Emily was a born minder, and like many timid people, Agnes knew she would fight with no holds barred to protect the one she cared about. Longbow's days of leggy blonde showgirls were coming to an end whether he realised it at this moment or not.

Longbow, still in a definitely dazed state, stayed up long after they returned to Mrs Nelligan's cottage.

'That girl could make a fortune in the States. It's the darnedest thing ever – Gaelic Flamenco!' he told Agnes.

'She is a most gentle girl, Jonas, and would need to be protected,' said Mrs Nelligan carefully, occupying herself with pouring another coffee for her ex-pupil.

'Yeah,' Longbow agreed thoughtfully. 'She sure is unlike any girl I ever met in America – or anywhere else, for that matter. Do you know, she actually blushes!' he smiled with the besotted look that told Mrs Nelligan that Emily would not have to wait too long before she would have a permanent protector, not to say a caring husband who would probably guide her vocal career to dizzy heights if she wished him to.

'Hackstown would be such a pretty place for a honeymoon, don't you think?' she said gently, and Longbow winked happily.

'Billy Markey is to have the house ready for me within six weeks – I reckon that would be long enough for any female to get her gear together ...' Then he suddenly stopped horrified by a dreadful thought. 'Mrs Nelligan, she hasn't got a steady fella has she? I wouldn't be cutting in on someone else who might be important to her?'

Mrs Nelligan shook her head reassuringly. 'I am sure I would have heard about it, if there was anyone serious in Emily's life; Lizzie would have mentioned it. But the best way to find out is to ask Emily herself which you can do tomorrow. Now, Jonas, do go to bed. Tomorrow is going to be another busy day for all of us.'

And in a corner of the Dungeon Disco, deaf to the roar of the rock music which Gerald was playing from the bank of equipment in the innermost room where, fortunately, the three-foot-thick walls kept the sound within and caused no disturbance to the district or to his father's resident clientele, Emily sat. Her eyes were closed and she was dizzy with contentment. Emily was in love – permanently, completely and irrevocably – and by four a.m. she had decided that some way she was going to fix things so that she could just be within vision range of her idol. She vowed she would follow Longbow to the ends of the earth, just to look on him from afar, which small ambition she felt she would have to be content with. She was, therefore, totally incoherent next day when Longbow drove up to where she was camped with her friends, packed her into his car and sped with her out to the house he had bought from Billy, so that he could tell her of his plans for its eventual rebirth into his dream house. When he asked her to marry him, Emily could do no more than nod speechlessly, holding his hand in total wonderment.

'I'm going to make you a household name in the States. You're going to be famous as the first Gaelic Flamenco singer ever,' he told her. 'We'll both top the bill and you'll have a special section in the show with a top-class flamenco musical backing. I'll go on tour again, just to look after you.'

Emily smiled, 'I'd rather just take care of you, Jonas,' she said shyly. 'I don't think I'm cut out to be a performer, and I only sing that way for fun. Anyway, Irish flamenco singing sounds pretty crazy when you think about it!'

'But that's just the point,' said Longbow excitedly. 'It's because it is quite daft that it's bound to take off. That's showbiz.'

And those who, six months later, were lucky enough to obtain tickets for the glittering extravaganza that launched Emily, by now re-christened 'Amalia O'Flaherty' into instant super-stardom, had to agree that it was, indeed, truly showbiz. And if the only people who didn't enthuse about it were the Spanish population, the Portuguese were loudly encouraging, living, obviously, in the fervent hope that Emily would never discover their beloved Fado.

Chapter Sixteen

The following eighteen months could be said to be idyllic for Hackstown. Into the third tourist season, Tir na n-Og was a runaway success with an actual waiting-list of would-be visitors on standby for any cancellations which might arise. Most of the American investors felt compelled to visit the complex which their goodwill and spare dollars had helped to build.

Even Mr 'Torch' Donelli, having made, from a business point of view, what could have been considered a fruitless journey, since the hamburger and space-game franchises had long been apportioned, nevertheless found plenty to entertain him, not least being a nubile young thing from West Cork who was working as a masseuse in the leisure complex's Teach Allis, or Sweat House – an ancient concept of sauna bathing, now modernised by Mr Okami. In fact, Mr Donelli was so taken with the ancient system of cleansing the body that he was seriously thinking of taking the whole idea to America and setting up a specialised complex of Irish sweat houses, just as long as the sweet young thing from West Cork would go along and run them for him. This proved a little more costly than he anticipated; she had three large-sized brothers back at home from whom, in the end, she refused to be parted, and Mr Donelli had to bring the lot of them to the United States with their young sister with the massage expertise. It turned out quite satisfactory really. The Familia took a good look at the boys and promptly recruited them into the Organisation where, after an initial period of playing Minders, they graduated into senior management in the construction industry and married good Italian virgins and raised large, law-abiding families. Their sister, however, had to contend with Mr

169

Donelli's Laurie Mae, who could see no valid reason why any Irish muscle pounder should interfere with what was a very comfortable gig for Laurie Mae. A subsequent showdown caused an unfortunate accident by way of a fracture to young Eileen's left arm, though Laurie Mae was sorry enough to drive her to the nearest hospital where a young intern with a solid Irish background did repair work. In due course he managed to wean Eileen away from the massage business and into running a medical practice which he obtained down in Louisiana. But by then Torch had sold the franchise for the sweat houses to a German entrepreneur anyway, and he was quite happy to remain faithful to Laurie Mae.

Mrs Nelligan, of course, was fully occupied keeping a guiding hand over the affairs of Tir na n-Og. She nevertheless had time to take a trip or two back to New York to visit Katie whose friendship with Jonathan Hogan was totally non-progressive as far as Agnes could ascertain. They quarrelled incessantly and she was almost tempted to give up on them completely. For how could you make two wooden-headed, arrogant, autocratic, independent, stubborn, impossible people come to terms with the fact that they were absolutely right for each other simply because they differed so much as to be basically totally alike! Katie was louder than ever in her belief that female emancipation was only gained without the encumbrance of a husband and family. Jonathan was equally insistent that marriage was a full-time career, not to be relegated to whatever time could be spared for it in between running a shop or designing clothes for rich fat women. Neither seemed prepared to move even a bit sideways not to mention backing down; even Daniel had given up on his son, for when he took Agnes out to dinner, he refused to mention the subject. In a very short time indeed, therefore, he learned quite a bit about Mrs Agnes Nelligan and she about Mr Daniel Hogan.

It was after one of her visits that she returned home to find the country plunged into a new General Election. Charlie Donaghue was back fighting for his governmental seat, and Gerald, whose Dungeon Disco had been so successful that he had recently opened Dungeon Disco Number Two, decided that he would join the political race on a youth ticket. His campaign was being expertly handled by the beautiful Lizzie who, as a literary personality and best-selling author, thanks to Mrs Nelligan's 'boy' in American publishing, was much in demand as a television speaker, radio commentator, and social and environmental affairs expert. Gerald and Charlie were not in opposition to each other, so it was a considerable satisfaction to Hackstown that when the election was over the village had not one, but two sitting governmental representatives to its name.

The village had taken to the high life with great ease. It was heartening to see the number of BMWs and Porsches which turned up in the Square for Friday shopping days at the supermarkets – and they were only the second cars for many of the local families. The hotel had undergone a major face-lift and now boasted of a French Bistro restaurant with a real French chef in attendance (Gerald would not tolerate any imitations of the genuine article.) Mrs Quinlan herself still attended to the hotel dining room food, though she now had four assistant chefs to take the workload. The Castle Court's reputation as a leading gourmet spot was firmly based on her home cooking and she was smart enough to realise that this was where the real regular clientele wanted to keep its patronage.

It all seemed to be so perfect, that it caused considerable shock waves when, one Tuesday morning, Charlie arrived in the hotel lounge for the usual eleven o'clock drinks date, looking as distrait as he had done when the Americans had first pulled out of Hackstown before the fortunes of the village had taken such an upturn.

Again, a sympathetic Matt put Charlie's usual brandy beside his elbow and Charlie downed it in a single swallow.

'Do you know what I heard in the House last night?' he said, his voice trembling with emotion. Matt slid a refill across the counter. 'You won't believe me when I tell you – it's such a total disaster.'

'Don't tell me we have to face another General Election already,' quipped Billy Markey who was inclined to believe that at times Charlie was given to pushing the panic button for no good reason.

'It's worse than that – at least it is for Hackstown,' said Charlie. 'You know that when we were out of office, the other lot had an agreement with a Dutch company to explore for oil off the Irish coast? Sure, didn't they beggar the exchequer shovin' the taxpayers' money into the project so that if the company did find anything worthwhile the Irish government would be able to claim the major share of it?'

'Well, what of it? If it wasn't the other lot doing oil explorations, your crowd would have us into a nuclear reactor in no time,' said Matt calmly, but Charlie brushed his comment aside.

'That's as may be, but the thing is, they actually had a good strike a month ago, and the government is keeping it dark to avoid speculative buying of the stock.'

'What you mean is, the boys want to get their own brokers on the job before the rest of us can raise the few bob for investment!' sniffed Billy.

'Well,' explained Charlie, breathlessly, 'the situation now is that they are planning on piping that oil right across the country into Dublin and from there up north. The pipeline will go in a run that cuts out their having to buy up tracts of agricultural land from the farmers – you know how they could hold up completion if they had a mind to.'

'Well, how does all this affect us here in Hackstown, Charlie?' asked Mrs Nelligan as she put down her coffee cup in its saucer, and settled back in her chair to give Charlie her entire attention. She could see that the Hackstown local representative was trying to get somewhere, and all that was needed was a little patience before all would be revealed.

'When they agreed to the development franchise, the other lot had a number of contingency plans drawn up and so had the developers, so that in the event of them finding anything worthwhile, they could pipe it to the most suitable transport outlet for the least cost.

'Now I had a bit of business in the Minister's office yesterday, and while I was there, I just happened to get a quick look at the plan which the Dutch marked as being the most practical to adopt from the point of view of direction and mileage economy between the strike and the outlets.' Charlie swallowed several times, before he continued.

'The bloody pipeline is scheduled to go right through our Tir na n-Og complex! It can cut off a roundabout of forty miles which is a hell of a saving of money and I understand that the Minister is going to slap a compulsory purchase order on the complex, if he doesn't decide to nationalise it first. Either way, he'll end up getting the place.'

There was a horrified silence in the lounge. Everyone could see what would happen; the river of revenue would dry up, the village would become a ghost town, and the high life enjoyed by Hackstown would cease for ever.

'But can they do this to us?' cried Mrs Pearson. 'Surely we have some rights? After all, the American President's wife did give us the land.'

'Where the demand for oil is so urgent, that's the only right anyone will recognise,' said Matt Quinlan. 'They'll claim that what they do is for the good of the majority and the country in general. How will Hackstown co-op argue that one away?'

'They'll pay a certain amount of hard cash over to compensate us for taking the complex away,' said Charlie.

'It's not the money that is important; it's having an industry in Hackstown that belongs to everyone which is the really valuable thing,' said Mrs Nelligan sadly.

'Can't they take an alternative route and bypass Hackstown?' asked Marjorie.

Charlie shook his head. 'Apart from the forty-mile roundabout which no one in their right mind would agree to, the only other economic route would take them right through Tara and the medieval remains designated as being our national heritage. No Minister could, or would, shove a dirty great pipeline through those,' he told his audience.

'My God!' said Billy angrily. 'We should never have let your lot get into government – now look at what's happened!'

Mrs Nelligan gave a little cough, and instinctively the others turned towards her.

'Charlie, how long have we got before the Minister starts

to publicise the whole situation of the pipeline and its route through Hackstown's Tir na n-Og?' she asked.

Charlie thought a moment. 'I'd say we have about three weeks give or take a week. The House is due to rise for the Easter recess in three days' time, and he won't get around to doing much about it until we convene again after the holidays.'

'Excellent,' Mrs Nelligan smiled. She turned to Matt Quinlan. 'Mr Quinlan, will you get on the telephone and book me the next available flight to New York, and I think you had better book a seat for Mr Markey also. I have a plan which may prove effective.'

The company visibly relaxed, while Matt hurried away to do her bidding. Billy didn't even ask what his function in America would be, any more than make a protest that his business might not manage to do without him. He trusted Mrs Nelligan's instincts completely and indeed he immediately began to look forward to the flight; Billy was not a man for overseas travel and this would be his first trip outside his own country.

Mr Quinlan returned, his mission satisfactorily accomplished. Then he poured them all drinks, providing Mrs Nelligan with her favourite pale dry sherry, and he carefully turned up the 'Closed' sign on the door of the lounge.

Mrs Nelligan sipped daintily from her glass. Then she put it down on the table beside her. She opened her briefcase and removed a somewhat ornately printed envelope from it. The flap carried a most impressive-looking crest in brilliant scarlet and gold, and the same crest was repeated on the letter-heading when Mrs Nelligan unfolded the sheet of paper the envelope contained.

'This is a communication I received recently from one of my old boys, Sheik Sayed Karim of Quatesh – he heads a sizeable oil consortium out there, as a matter of fact. I had him for a couple of years at my Academy; a delightful boy and beautifully mannered. It was a pleasure to teach him. I remember he had quite a pleasant singing voice too,' she said reminiscently. Marjorie stirred a little restlessly in her anxiety, and Mrs Nelligan came back from her pleasant reveries of the past.

'Now Sayed has asked me if I knew of any good investment his group could interest themselves in over here. He always liked Ireland and he would like a good-sized property of some sort in this country. It could provide facilities for holidays, conferences, functions, meetings and so on, he says.'

Then she took out a second envelope, this time a business-like missive in discreet black and green heading. 'By a strange coincidence, the Associates of American Democracy have also displayed a keen interest in placing their combined investment portfolio here as well. The Friendly Sons of St Brigid contacted my nephew Roger and asked if he could come up with something solidly blue chip for them over here. And it now strikes me that we might run a little auction between the Associates and Sayed's consortium and sell off Tir na n-Og to one or other of them.'

'How splendid!' cried Geoffrey delightedly. 'Mrs Nelligan, you are a positive genius! After all, big business must take its own risks when it goes into the market place. It will be up to the bidders to find out for themselves how gilt-edged the property will remain.'

Mrs Nelligan looked shocked. 'My dear Mr Pearson, you surely don't imagine I would allow these people to buy the complex without acquainting them of the possible takeover by the government? Why, that would be nothing short of fraud, and I certainly would not condone it. And I would never risk Mr Markey's career through making him a party to such a deceit.'

Geoffrey looked suitably chastened. 'Do forgive me, Mrs Nelligan. I simply did not think it through. Of course, you must tell them what the government has in mind. But won't that effectively put paid to your making a sale to either of the parties concerned?'

'Not at all,' replied Mrs. Nelligan gently. 'The kind of advance knowledge they will obtain from me will be most useful to them, if and when they do bid against each other.' She finished her sherry, stood up and delicately inclined her head in farewell to the others, and then betook herself back home to pack.

175

Chapter Seventeen

After they reached New York, the week that followed proved a busy one for Mrs Nelligan and Billy. There were numerous meetings between the interested bidders and the vendors of Hackstown's Tir na n-Og. The Associates of American Democracy and its companion, the Friendly Sons of St Brigid, were represented (much to Billy's surprise, since he was not, at the start of negotiations, acquainted with the affiliations of both societies) by a trio of mohair-suited Mediterranean-type whizz kids, whose brief-cases came in the finest of tooled leather with gold clasps and initialling, and which were filled with bulky files of columned figures. They seemed to know a great deal about the workings of Hackstown's complex and were full of praise for the accountancy system used by Miss Kitty Dermody, from whom they had received the statements of accounts on instruction from the co-operative committee.

Mrs Nelligan herself handled the Arab consortium. Young Sheik Sayed wined and dined her almost every evening, while Billy was coping with the Associates and the Friendly Sons group, and when they met and exchanged progress reports, it was obvious that the final auction was going to be hotly contested. Billy, who had been carefully coached by Mrs Nelligan on how to deal with the proposed governmental measures in his conversations with the Associates, assured Mrs Nelligan that the team of whizz kids was fully prepared to deal effectively with the pipeline plans, should its final bid for the complex succeed. And for her part she was satisfied that Sayed's consortium would see the problem as no more than a fly to be swatted and ignored, if they could outbid the Mafia, the Sons and the Associates, combined.

'My dear Mrs Nelligan, you know it could be most

important to us that we obtain the complex,' said Sayed as they sat over their coffee after a meal in one of New York's most elegant restaurants the night before the auction.

'Sayed, you know nothing would please me more than to see the complex in your hands, but you will have to fight for it with hard cash. The Associates are most anxious to buy into Ireland under the guise of the Friendly Sons of St Brigid – they need a convenient laundering place for their money, it would appear.'

Sayed made a dismissive gesture. 'But they would bring in gambling machines, clubs, illegal games of chance and who knows what else, if they were to outbid us,' he said. 'They could even turn Hackstown into a Las Vegas within a year.'

Mrs Nelligan nodded. 'But they have the right to bid. We cannot refuse their offer at auction.'

'We will better it, come what may,' Sayed said firmly. 'We see the complex as an ideal investment but also as a most suitable holiday venue for our families, apart from its being most useful for business purposes. We would install a helicopter port, of course, and there would have to be a small mosque, but apart from that, things would be left as they are in every aspect. The co-operative would continue to run things as before.'

Then Sayed took her hand in his, and looked at her with his old affection. 'When this is all concluded, my friend, I will have a special request for you and I hope you will accede to it,' he told her. And though she gently probed, Sayed would say nothing more.

Agnes had advised the First Lady of the new situation, and for her part, the First Lady was putting her money on Sayed. The whole thing would, she told her husband, make for good relations between the Arab countries and the United States, if one looked at it in the right perspective. And though he didn't quite follow her reasoning – not that he often did – the President decided he should agree with his wife's thinking. She usually turned out to be right. Anyway, he couldn't stand those goddammed Italians – always yattering and ponging of garlic, to which he had a deep-rooted aversion, ever since he had been posted to Rome early in his political career.

To keep an eye on things, however, the First Lady sent down 'Jimmy' James Stafford and instructed him to report to her instantly by diplomatic telephone, should anything go wrong on the day.

At five o'clock precisely, Mr Billy Markey ascended the dais in the Hotel Conrad, feeling unaccountably nervous, which surprised him, for after all, Billy had seen a great deal of good property go through his professional hands. Many thousands of good Irish farmland came under his hammer over the years. But this was different – he was about to work a deal that would affect the lifestyle of his own village for years to come and it was up to him to wheedle the best possible figure he could from a group who were so hard-headed in business that they made Billy feel like a total amateur, which was saying a mouthful, Billy having a well-deserved reputation for being able to extract the extra thousand or two from a dead man, if he had to. But it was going to be a new experience for Billy to accept bids in millions rather than in hundreds, and he hoped he would not fall down on the job.

'Right, now, gentlemen, and ladies present,' Billy began with a nervous smile. 'We have for auction a superb investment property ideally situated in the heart of scenic Ireland. The first year's turnover came close to double the expected target, and the projections over the next five years, all going well, could see a growth rate which would make this investment as good as gilt edged.'

Mrs Nelligan coughed warningly, and Billy came down from his enthusiastic flight of descriptive fancy.

'You will have seen the brochure and you must be aware of the potential for expansion of the existing amenities, and you have been informed of the possible new developments which government intervention may create –'

He was summarily interrupted by one of the mohair-suited ones, who obviously boasted of more shine than polish. 'We got all that – let's start the bidding. Time is dollars and cents, OK?' He smiled toothily over at Sayed who sat with his advisors at the other side of the room. Sayed nodded politely and flicked a finger at one of his companions.

The second representative of the Associates of American Democracy made the opening bid.

'Three mill,' he said, flashing his well-tailored teeth at Billy.

'I assume that is just an opening bid?' said Billy with his usual initial auctioneer's disdain.

Sayed's advisor moved his little finger.

'Your bid has just been doubled, sir,' said Billy, calm suddenly descending upon him.

'Up a half,' said the mohair-suited one and Sayed nodded at his companion again.

'The offer is up another million,' said Billy, making careful notes on his pad.

There was a slight pause while the whizz kids conferred.

'And another half,' said the bidder with somewhat less assurance. Another flick from the Arabian corner and Billy announced the gauge was up by yet another million.

'And twenty-five thousand,' said the Associates bidder, but Billy would have none of it.

'Bids must be made in half-million amounts from now on, gentlemen,' he announced with some satisfaction, as he calculated that the running price so far on Hackstown's fairyland was nine and a half million American dollars.

'Now, you're not going to lose the property for a mere half-million dollars, are you?' Billy asked the Associates of American Democracy, with some mischievousness. He hadn't exactly taken to the whizz kids who had tried to downgrade his abilities in no small way, every time he had to meet them. They collectively glowered at him and one asked for a five-minute recess while he phoned his principals. Billy obligingly halted the proceedings while the bidder dashed outside and contacted his bosses on his call phone, and then after some mumbling he returned somewhat chastened and announced they would go another million and no more.

Sayed looked down his well-shaped Arab nose at the trio and nodded to his bidder, and with considerable delight, Billy accepted a closing bid of another two million dollars, and Hackstown Tir na n-Og became the property of the Quatesh Consortium.

Amid considerable excitement, Daniel and his television

crew immediately moved in from their places at the back of the room where they had been quietly filming the proceedings and organised an interview with the unsuccessful team from the Sons and the Associates.

'Our Irish members will be real disappointed. We had hoped to secure the complex for the Irish Americans who regarded it as their piece of ground in their home country,' commented one of the mohaired ones, with suitably mournful expression.

'How would you have coped with the pipeline situation?' asked Daniel whose expression was growing more sceptical while the whizz kid was speaking.

'We'd have paid to have the pipeline diverted so as to avoid the complex completely – there's plenty of land we could buy over. We'd have been happy to save the green and pleasant country for the Irish rather than see it go to ... foreigners.' said the second mohair suit. 'And of course, we'd have developed that complex into a real viable property: a pleasure-dome, a carnival site and even a nice casino. Everyone woulda made money.' Daniel nodded and then turned his cameras on the Arabs who were smilingly shaking hands with Billy and Mrs Nelligan in obvious delight and satisfaction.

He tackled Sayed who was still holding the diamond-encrusted gold pen with which he had just signed the percentage payment cheque.

'And what are you planning to do with Hackstown's Tir na n-Og, Sheik Sayed?' he asked. Sayed smiled into the cameras.

'Do?' he said. 'Why, nothing! We will use it as it is intended to be used, for holidays and happy times and it will continue to be run by the present committee and the village. We will build a helicopter port or perhaps a small airstrip for holiday flights at budget rates for tourists. Hackstown does not need us to move in and change it around; its committee have done a superb job without any outsider wanting to alter it.'

'But what about the pipeline?' asked Daniel. 'Won't that change the place anyhow?'

Sayed looked firmly at Daniel. 'There will be no pipeline

180

running through Hackstown leisure complex, of that I can assure you,' he said.

A small pressure of his well-shod foot prevented Daniel from pursuing the question of pipelines and governmental commitments for cheaper power for the Irish population.

Daniel was, therefore, totally unsurprised when, some weeks later, an announcement from the Irish Government Press office advised the public that the recent oil strike in the Celtic sea had been found to be merely a pocket which would not prove viable to develop. And when a further news story emerged concerning a particularly favourable agreement to supply oil to the country at a cost which was practically classifiable as money from home, Daniel did not have to do too much research to find out that the company providing the bonanza was a well-buried subsidiary of the Quatesh consortium which was making sure that not only was its Irish holiday investment property safe from intervention, but that its national industry, which was providing the cash to pay for its pleasures, was effectively cutting out potential competition. True, the Dutch were not over-pleased, but then, if one were prepared to give a little here and bend a little there, items of negotiation in a troubled commercial world were not difficult to uncover, when one looked for them.

The consortium had no real wish to go into active business, being content to leave the running of Tir na n-Og to the locals as long as it had free access and a reasonable percentage return for an eleven and a half million dollar investment. After all, oil production being what it was in Quatesh, they had absolutely nothing on which to spend the golden millions. As Sayed reminded Mrs Nelligan, they were a small country, and one could only build so many palaces, fund so many hospitals and schools, and besides the population was sparse and well scattered, and it had no desire to be propelled into the twentieth century simply because a hole in the ground produced a liquid they themselves had no use for in the living conditions they favoured.

Only Major Mulqueen was unhappy. He missed the Gun Club and the status it had given him. It simply was not the same being a guest at someone else's club and he found time hanging heavily on his hands, now that he had not the Club paperwork to attend to as before.

When he was told about the sale of the complex to the Arabs, he was outraged.

'I knew that no good would come of this whole damn project,' he said loudly in the lounge of the Castle Court. 'Now we'll have a crowd of wogs in the country!'

'The Arabs are not wogs, Major, they are extremely cultivated people,' remonstrated Marjorie Pearson.

'Wogs, wops, what's the difference? You can't trust any of 'em. I never found one of those savages worth a damn on the parade ground,' the Major snorted.

'Funny, I never knew the Irish army had Arab personnel,' said Matt Quinlan, who knew full well that the Major's service had been achieved entirely within his own country, between the wars, he having been said to have had a faulty ear-drum when units were dispatched to keep the peace in other areas overseas.

Major Mulqueen chose to ignore him. 'You'll see – they'll have gangs of wives roaming around the place. Next thing you know they'll be importing drugs and camels into the village. You couldn't be up to them.'

He stamped out, almost knocking down a bespectacled stout little man clad in jodhpurs and high-necked yellow pullover, who was on his way into the hotel. The Major glared at him and then, recognising him, gave a gruff apology, pausing for a moment to address the new arrival.

'Heard the latest that lot have done?' he said crossly, jerking a thumb towards the lounge. 'You can say goodbye to your standard of living from now on. People like you and me have no say these days.' He disappeared out the door and the little man joined the drinkers around the bar.

Matt recognised him for one of the more recent arrivals into the district, a retired British foreign service official, whose diplomatic career in India had been unmarked by any achievement other than the development of a total revulsion of anything or anyone foreign, coloured, native or non-British. He wasn't too keen on the Irish either, so it was quite a surprise to find him about to fraternise in the Castle

182

Court lounge. He ordered a gin and bitters, and sat in the corner of the bar, sipping his drink as he leafed through his newspaper which, from its title, Matt knew wasn't obtainable in Hackstown, which meant he had it specially ordered from Dublin. Which told Matt the stout man would always be what an Irish Prime Minister had once termed 'A Blow In'.

'I say,' the stout man began accusingly. 'Is it true that you've gone and sold your leisure complex to a bunch of Arab wallahs?'

'What if it is – sir? It's still a free market,' said Matt with commendable restraint as he concentrated his attentions on repolishing an already immaculate counter top.

'Goddam stupid thing to do, if you ask me. It'll lower the tone of the entire district,' said the little man, taking a gulp from his gin.

'We've never had a complaint about the tone of the area until now,' said Billy, frantically endeavouring to place this aggressive stranger, whose face just kept edging out from the edge of his memory.

'Well, *I'm* damn well complaining. I didn't put my money into a property to have to exist side by side with a bunch of heathens. I suppose you know they start keening at Mecca five times a day?'

'We have always believed in the benefits of religious freedom in Hackstown,' said Marjorie defensively. 'As one of the minority, I have never experienced religious bias, so why should I encourage it elsewhere? If the new owners wish to practise their religious cultures, I am sure the village will quite understand.'

'Maybe they won't understand so easily when these people arrive with twenty or thirty concubines in their harems and start trying to buy your local maidens for a couple of sheep,' retorted the stout man, gesturing for a refill of his gin and bitters.

'You have an experience of their culture?' asked Geoffrey with distaste, for he had taken an instant dislike to the little man – he knew rank colonialism when he met it, with or without a pink gin in hand.

'Ten years in India, eight in Cairo, British Colonial

183

Service in the days when we had an Empire for the sun to set on.'

'You don't care for foreigners?' Geoffrey asked.

'Never trusted 'em – never found cause to change my mind about 'em. Lazy, dishonest, liars all of them. Won't learn English for the most part, and pretend they don't understand you when they do.'

Silently, Mr Quinlan placed his drink before him and the stout man took a swallow.

'When I found the way Britain was allowing all those wallahs into the country from God knows where, I decided it was time for me to leave. So I had my agent buy me a place over here. At least you Irish are more or less like us and you speak the same tongue, even if you do manage to bend it slightly.' He chortled, ignoring the sudden freeze that descended on the drinkers.

Billy suddenly clicked into recognition.

'You bought Moorfield Farm, didn't you? he asked.

The man nodded. 'Wasn't concerned too much about living next to the complex. I felt I'd meet some of my own kind who would be taking holidays there. The new situation is a totally different kettle of fish.' He clumped down the glass on the bar counter. 'Have to rethink my position now – definitely. Can't see myself remaining at Moorfield. Damn nuisance really – quite liked it.' He slid off the stool and trotted briskly out of the lounge at a fast pace. There was a small silence when he had gone.

'It looks as if we are about to lose that delightful gentleman as a resident,' said Geoffrey with considerable disgust.

Mrs Nelligan nodded. 'Billy,' she said, 'you ought to see if he is interested in selling his property back to you. I have an idea as to how we could turn his distaste of foreigners to our advantage.'

Which accounts for how the Hackstown Tir na n-Og co-operative managed to administer the unkindest cut of all to the good Major Mulqueen.

Two days later, Billy was in a position to advise Mrs Nelligan and her committee that he could close the deal on Moorfield Farm for them without any hassle. The property consisted of the farmhouse and about one hundred acres, give or take. In fact the ex-colonial owner was more than happy to sell with a modest profit margin, now that he had definitely decided he had no wish to live cheek by jowl with a community of what he called 'middle-eastern infidels'. In fact, he could hardly wait to sign the papers, pocket his cheque and return to his newest bolt hole – the northern reaches of Scotland. He was only a month installed in an isolated lake-side manor when he discovered to his dismay that the local laird was an Indian gentleman, with the unlikely name of Kassim MacGregor by an odd twist of inheritance.

'Splendid,' said Mrs Nelligan. 'I thought it would be a fine gesture for the co-operative to purchase the land and then offer it to the Hackstown Gun Club at a peppercorn rent. Then the Major could resume his old way of life and we would have the pleasure of having him for ever more under a compliment to Hackstown's Tir na n-Og!'

'What's more,' chuckled Matt above the sudden burst of clapping which greeted Mrs Nelligan's naughty but justified point of view. 'If he steps out of line, we can always threaten to cancel his lease!'

Mrs Nelligan shook her head reprovingly. 'Now Mr. Quinlan,' she said gently. 'Do bear in mind the importance of the little maxim I always gave to my boys: "Forbearance in Victory". We must hope that Major Mulqueen will have learned something from the past year and make no plans to exact retribution from him by way of humiliations – any more than is absolutely necessary of course.'

And her smile would have chilled the heart of the KGB.

Epilogue

A few weeks after the auction in New York, Sayed paid a call on Hackstown where he was received with pleasure and some ceremony by the residents. Even the Major, who had been invited to the formal dinner Sayed gave before he returned to America, was quite polite. He had been remarkably even tempered now that he was back organising the new Gun Club: contacting old members, arranging shoots, having stock ordered, hides made for the use of members, and all the new ideas he was at last in a position to put into operation to make the new club one of the best in the county. He grudgingly agreed that the fella was quite passable and well mannered – even if he would never permit his sister to marry one of them. And since the Major's only sister was forty-five, single, and living happily pursuing her chosen career in civil engineering, the possibility would never arise, so Mrs Mulqueen ignored him and picked out one of her most charming antiques – a beaten silver amulet for Sayed to bring home to his wife as a gift from the Mulqueen antiques shop.

The banquet had been given in the hall of Illan Castle, under a portrait of the First Lady and her husband the President. In an alcove at the far end of the enormous hall, now removed from its plinth so that it was a more manageable size, stood Alvin's statue, which had at last been given a purpose in life. Cleaned of all the bird droppings and relieved of the magpies' nest, it made an excellent coat rack since each spiked section could accommodate six coat hangers. The haggis-type lumps around the base were given little electric bulbs set into the tin lids and the whole thing lit up like a Christmas tree. And the enterprising banqueting manager wired up the two bird figures into an automatic audio unit over which he had baroque music broadcast while the patrons were dining. It was a tremendous success with everyone because of its sheer bad taste!

'Mrs Nelligan,' said Sayed, as they sat in the flickering candlelight of the banquet hall. 'You will remember I told you at the auction that I would have a special request to make of you?'

'I do indeed, my dear Sayed,' replied his ex-teacher with affection. 'And if I can accede to it, you know I will be most happy to do so.'

'Oh I hope you will,' said Sayed earnestly. 'What I want more than anything, is for you to come back to America with me and teach my two sons for one year. We will be remaining in New York for about twelve months more before I must return to Quatesh, and my wife and I would be most gratified if you would ensure that our children receive the kind of values that will be essential to their future positions as rulers of their country, so that they may govern it wisely. I know of only one person to instil such values into them, and that is your good self.'

Mrs Nelligan smiled brilliantly at him. 'You do me a great honour, putting your sons into my care,' she said. 'Allow me to give the matter some thought for a little while.'

She had a feeling she would say yes to his suggestion and a small ripple of anticipation went through her. A whole year would be nice in New York, particularly if Daniel Hogan were around to relax with. Which of course brought her back again to Katie and Jonathan.

And suddenly, the whole solution came to her. A lengthy phone-call to 'Bobo' Carter of West Coast Tran-Tel Incorporated, and Jonathan had an offer to make a major film on the Company's behalf about the life and family of the First Lady, using Hackstown and Illan Castle as background. Jonathan was offered total control of what turned out to be a highly romantic and inventive story indeed which pleased the First Family no end and didn't do Bobo too much harm in the political arena in the long run either. Bobo, like the well-trained old boy of Mrs Nelligan's that he was, made, on suggestion from his ex-teacher, only one condition: that Miss Katie O'Carroll, alias 'Katinka', would design the costumes for the film, and to that, Jonathan had to agree.

By the end of a month, he found that working with Katie was pure inspiration and he simply could not see himself going back to the old arrangement of being employed by someone else. It was only a short step to establishing his own production company which was to prove one of the success stories of the television business and ultimately the most creative husband and wife team in the profession. And in between times, Katie managed to produce twin girls who ruled Jonathan with chubby iron fists from the moment they arrived on the scene.

And the only plan with which Mrs Nelligan was not yet acquainted was a little scheme Sayed was keeping up his sleeve. Once the complex became the regular venue of his compatriots, Sayed planned to open an exclusive school for the children of his peers, for whom the methods of big-business multi-nationals, conglomerates and corporations would be a way of life.

And who, he asked himself, would be better to perfect them in the arts of survival, than his ex-mentor, Mrs Agnes Nelligan?

Except that no one thought to advise him that he might well have some opposition to his plan to engage Agnes to head his scholastic establishment, from a man named Daniel Hogan.